CROSSING the LINE

KARLA DOYLE

COPYRIGHT

ISBN 9780992152710
(Digital Edition ISBN: 9780992152703)

Cover by Emily Ugarenko
Cover photography by Curaphotography, Bart78/Bigstockphoto

Electronic book publication November 2013
Print book publication November 2013

For questions and comments about this book, please contact the author at <u>karla@karladoyle.com</u>.

Acknowledgements

Without these people, this book would still be sitting in the half-finished folder.

For my hubby, Todd, who supports and believes in everything I do, wholeheartedly. I love you forever.

For Amanda, my amazing (and incredibly tolerant) bestie. Thank you. For everything, but mostly for making me laugh. I'll never be able to look at thick, sturdy carrots without hearing your voice. I don't ever want to do a book without you.

For Andie. You keep me sane, and we both know that's no small task! I'm so thankful fate put us together in NYC and you're part of my life.

To Skye—thank you for answering my many questions and holding my hand through this entire process. You're a fantastic editor and a lovely friend.

Thank you, Emily, for the fabulously hot cover. I can't wait for you to design another.

Thanks also to Leigh, Gwen, Claire, and Em. Much gratitude, all.

TABLE OF CONTENTS

Chapter One

"Fucking ties. What idiot invented these things?" Derrick snapped the strip of gray silk from its stranglehold around his neck. "To hell with it, not doing it," he said, launching the thing at a garbage can.

His best friend Jeremy raised his dark eyebrows but he left the tie where it'd landed. "I have a solution. We pretend I won the coin toss that night. I get the girl, you get to avoid the marital noose."

"Yeah, not happening. Hanna's all mine and that's the way it's gonna stay, 'til death do us part. Longer than that if my deal with the devil holds." He nodded at the can. "Grab that stupid fucking thing for me. I've got an angel to marry."

Took a few more tries, a hell of a lot of cursing and some help from his best man, but he won the battle of the Windsor. Didn't mean he liked it though. He slid two fingers under his collar and popped the top button on his shirt. A little breathing room, at least. "I can't believe you wear one of these every day."

"You get used to it," Jeremy said, cinching his tie with ease.

"Not this guy. I'll stick with t-shirts and hardhats." He slid on the black jacket that completed the monkey suit he'd been assigned and checked out the results in the mirror. "But I do make this shit look good."

Jeremy laughed until Derrick made a beeline across the large, sunshine-filled room and opened the door.

"Hey, where're you going—we're supposed to wait here for the minister."

"Can't wait. Have to see my bride."

"One of her parents catches you and you'll be out of order for the wedding night."

"Not a problem. I've only been caught once, and that was by the woman I'm going to see."

"Hey, D..." Jeremy called as Derrick reached the opening. "Good luck, man."

Derrick nodded his thanks and stepped into the main floor of the Collins' house, Hanna's childhood home. The place was a mansion compared to the hole-in-the-wall house by the tracks where he'd grown up. If he'd known that night two years ago that Hanna came from money, he might've handed off the opportunity to ask her out to Jeremy, despite winning the coin toss. Derrick didn't date princesses. Didn't fuck them either. Until Hanna—his first and last. His forever girl.

Thanks to the ultra-plush carpeting that ran through the house, nobody heard him climbing the stairs. Or walking down the hall toward the last door on the left, Hanna's old bedroom. He'd have been happy to make things legal at some chapel in Niagara Falls, where she'd made him the happiest man alive by accepting his proposal.

But deny Hanna the pretty, garden wedding she'd dreamed about and deserved? No way. So here they were. And here he was, three steps from his bride-to-be's half-open door.

"It's not too late to call it off." Mrs. Collins' voice, in its usual, judgmental tone.

"Mom, please."

"Hanna, you need to listen to me."

All the muscles in his body seized. If anybody walked out of one of these second-floor rooms, he was fucked. Because he couldn't move. All he could do was listen, same as the woman he loved had just been ordered to do.

"Your dad and I know why you're doing this, marrying a scruffy, tattooed ruffian like Derrick."

"Because I love him. So glad you figured that out after almost two years."

With that, he could move again. And he did, closing the distance to the door by half.

Abigail Collins tsked, loudly and disapprovingly. He could picture the expression on her face. Sour, her favorite mask whenever he was around.

"You don't love him, you're infatuated. He's dirty and dangerous and it's exciting. But the excitement will fade, darling girl, and then you'll be stuck. Tied to a horrible family and a husband who'll have to go on disability or welfare when his body gives out because he has no other prospects beyond heavy lifting. Then what? You'll watch him drink himself into oblivion, the way his father always does? Maybe while you chase a couple of scruffy, disrespectful children around a ramshackle apartment?"

The muscle control he'd regained a minute earlier disappeared when Hanna didn't answer. Fuck. *Fuck.*

"Hanna." Abigail's voice had softened. "Let me tell the minister there won't be a wedding today. You can move back home immediately and, once you're settled, move on with the right kind of man. Like that Jeremy Cruz. Now he's a catch. Nice short hair and always clean-shaven—now he's a handsome man who'll make beautiful children. And he's from a lovely family, making a good career for himself. Nothing like—"

"Fucking stop, Mom. Just fucking stop."

"Hanna Marie Collins, you mind your foul mouth. You see the horrible influence he's had on you?"

Oh yeah, now he could move. To right outside that door, should his newly foul-mouthed fiancée require backup.

"You need to listen to *me*. You're right, being with Derrick is exciting, maybe even a little bit dangerous sometimes. And maybe that'll fade. If it does, I don't give a damn. That's one tiny part of him, of why I love him. You don't know him, all you see is the superficial stuff. Yes, he has tattoos and a motorcycle and he operates a jackhammer instead of sitting behind a desk. And yes, his dad is a piece of shit, but Derrick's not like his asshole father, just like I'm not like my giant bitch of a mother. So you listen to *me*, Mom, because this is the last time I'm having this conversation with you. I love Derrick and I'm marrying him. Today. I can do that in your backyard with all the pretty fixings that'll impress your friends, or in a two-minute long, late-night service in a Niagara Falls wedding chapel. Your call."

Derrick backed away even quieter than he'd approached. His strong, beautiful princess didn't need any backup. Her parents were right—she was too good for him. Could do fifty times better. One hundred times. Didn't matter, because she wanted *him*. They were going to bed tonight as husband and wife. After which he'd spend every day of his life worshipping her and never letting her go.

Chapter Two

"I want to talk to you about something." So much for thinking a while before saying anything. When his wife walked through the door in that short dress and high-heeled sandals that showed off her sexy legs, Derrick's second brain took over. All patience and planning went directly out the kitchen window.

"Sure, shoot." Mid-afternoon sunshine glinted off Hanna's long, auburn hair, giving her a golden, angelic aura. The hottest angel he'd ever seen smiled over her shoulder while loading the groceries into the fridge. On the counter sat a bag of thick carrots, a cucumber, a zucchini. Innocent vegetables, normally. Right now they all reminded him of cocks. And Hanna, deep-throating said cocks, which was one helluva smokin' visual.

"I used your computer while you were out."

"Is yours screwed again? Maybe it's time you got rid of it and bought a new one. We can take some money from our savings account."

The only word that really registered was *screwed*. Add that to the stuff on his mind and the hint of ass he saw when she bent, and he couldn't have stopped this conversation if he tried. "I was looking for a link to that little resort we talked about a few days ago. I checked your browsing history."

"Havenbrook? Did you find it—if not, I jotted it down."

Fuck, he was sweating, had a first-class woody, and she didn't have a clue. "Yeah, I got it."

"Great." She pushed a carton of eggs into place, closed the door and turned. "So what do you think, should we book a romantic weekend?"

Romantic might not be the word for what he had in mind. Fucking hot, absolutely, if this didn't explode in his face. "Know what else I found in your history— quite a few solo visits to our favorite X-rated website. You watched a lot of porn last week."

"I wouldn't say *a lot*." She must've been blushing pretty damn hard for him to see it through her summer-tanned skin. She toyed with the bottom of her dress, hiking it higher up her thighs until a glimpse of white panty showed. Teasing him, whether consciously or not. "No more than usual."

"I watched them," he stepped toward her, "the videos saved in your favorites." Another step and she was within touching distance, the heat between them flaring. "Did you get yourself off while you watched them?"

"You know I did."

Yeah, he did. Having a smart, hot wife who enjoyed porn fucking rocked. He was the luckiest guy on earth, coming home to Hanna every night, knowing he had her eager, willing body all to himself. So what the hell was he doing?

"Do you want to watch them with me right now?" Sparks skittered along his shoulder where her fingernails dragged a line. Her palms slid down his bare chest, into his shorts, and she smiled at what she found. "Mmm, rock hard—perfect for sucking." She pulled her hand out. Tortured him further by licking her fingertips. "I haven't come yet today. I've been waiting for you, like you told me to."

Eight years of marriage and things had only gotten hotter between them. This morning, he'd woken her by licking her, taking her to the edge but not finishing the job. Then he'd ordered her to suck him to the same point. Made her promise she wouldn't come until later, and he'd do the same. Delaying the gratification was one of his favorite games to play with her. The more they stoked the fire throughout the day, the wilder things got when they let loose. But the blue balls in his shorts were probably to blame for some of the stuff going through his head this afternoon.

"You cue up a video," her tongue slid along her plump bottom lip, "and I'll grab a few things from the bedroom."

So they could act out a three-way scene, something they both loved doing. But they could do better. "Not yet, I still want to talk to you." He hiked her dress up to her waist and slid his hand in the front of her tiny panties. So wet for him, for what they did to each other. "The videos you watch, the stuff we pretend — we can do that if you want. Really do it."

A couple of seconds ticked by before it clicked. "What...why? No, no, I don't need that. Just you, you're all I need."

Ah, there it was, the importance of a single word. She didn't *need* to be with two men at once, but she hadn't said she didn't *want* to be.

He circled her clit in the slow, but firm, way that he knew made her desperate for release. Had her clinging to his biceps, grinding on his hand in less than a minute. "But you'd like it, wouldn't you? To have one big cock down your throat while another one fucks you?"

"I'd never cheat on you. Never."

"I know that, baby, I do. But it wouldn't be cheating if I agreed, if I was the one fucking you while you sucked another guy's dick." Yeah, she shook her head, but he'd heard the hitch in her breathing, felt her pulse jump at his description. He reached over to the counter and snagged a thick, sturdy carrot from the bag, brought it to her mouth. "Think about it, how good it'd feel. Better than just watching and pretending, like this." He teased an inch of the carrot between her parted lips. Then another, before drawing it out. "That could be a real, flesh and blood cock. Forget need — I'm talking about want."

"Derrick…"

He guided her to their table — the one she'd paid ten bucks for at a yard sale, then spent a weekend watching him sand and paint. Every time he looked at the refinished table, he thought of Hanna, her thick hair pulled into a high ponytail that grazed her shoulder as she leaned on his workbench, wide-eyed and smiling. One of hundreds — no, thousands — of simple yet amazing memories they'd made. They were about to add another to the list. He stripped her of the dress and panties. No bra under the dress, just two perfect tits with very hard nipples. Fucking beautiful, his wife.

"Over you go. Spread your legs and show me where you want my cock." His gorgeous wife obeyed, giving him a primo view of glistening pink and just above, a tight little ring otherwise known as heaven. "Do you want me to fuck you here," he slid a finger inside her pussy, "or in your ass?"

"Yes and yes."

"See...you do want it all, don't you, baby?" At her whimpered yes, he shoved his shorts down past his hips. He settled the head of his dick at her entrance and leaned over her back, the thick carrot in his hand. "Hold this and suck it like the cock you wish it was. Keep it in there nice and deep while I make you come." It killed him not to thrust inside, to bury himself to the balls. But it'd be worth the wait – it always was. Right now, he wanted to watch.

Hanna stroked the carrot as she'd do to his cock if he were standing in front of her. She licked up and down its length, then eased the thing into her mouth. They'd done this plenty of times before with dildos. Whether his dick or sex toys or this impromptu veggie of the day, he loved watching her suck, the way her cheeks hollowed and her eyes squeezed closed when she couldn't take another fraction of an inch. The sight made him harder than a fucking battering ram.

She loved it too. Loved getting fucked while her mouth was full of shaft. Sometimes they'd reverse things, he'd fill her sweet pussy or ass – or both – with a plug or vibrator, then watch her go crazy sucking his cock. Judging by her solo porn preferences, she craved more than just a toy at one end. And call him fucked-up, but the idea of that, of Hanna blowing another man while he fucked her deep and hard, sent every last drop of blood surging to his cock.

He bent over her again, tucking her hair behind her ear so he could nibble the soft lobe before speaking. "I want you to do something for me." He grinned at her instant hum of compliance. "Pick somebody whose dick you'd like to suck – and mine doesn't count – and think of him while you work that carrot. Think of both of us while you come with it in your mouth." He straightened, then slid home. He stilled so he could watch her mouth, her face. As she fell into a sucking rhythm, he pulled out and thrust again. "Are you thinking of him, picturing him filling your mouth while I fuck you?"

A throaty *"mmmhmm"* drifted up.

Who had she chosen, who was she thinking about right now? A celebrity, one of the ultra-hung guys from the porn vids? Or somebody closer to home? Whoever it was, she was into it. Really fucking into it. Her head bobbed up and down on the make-believe dick and ten-thousand sparks shot straight to his balls. He had sixty seconds max before he lost it. He pulled out, scooped some of her juices and spread it over her ass. He reached between her legs and squeezed her clit between two fingers. At her muffled moan, he angled his cock higher and pushed inside.

"Fuck, baby, I love being in your tight little ass." So much, he had to grind his teeth together not to come as his last inch disappeared from view. Didn't matter how many times and ways he'd been inside her, each one still stripped him of control.

Her hips rocked against his hand. He rolled his fingers back and forth over her clit, giving her the pressure she needed. And she was almost there. He pulled back, slid home again, wanting to pound into her so fucking bad. Another time. He focused on her face instead. The would-be cock sliding in and out of her mouth. Her sounds as he rubbed her harder, as his hips smacked against her perfectly rounded ass.

Then it hit, her sexy moans filling the kitchen. Beneath him, she jerked and bucked, each grind of her hips causing her ass to tighten around his cock, nearly to the point of pain. But so hot. So fucking hot.

"Jesus, fuck…" His head fell back as he hollered, his pulse pounding in his ears, stars blinding his tightly closed eyes. "I love you, baby. So much," he said, collapsing on her back. "You know that, right?"

"I do. Pretty sure the neighbors know it too, since I can smell their barbecue through the open window."

He laughed against her hair, burying his face in its scent and silkiness. Wouldn't be the first time their sex sounds had escaped the house. "Want me to wander over and tell Brian I hit my finger with a hammer?"

"I think you've already used that excuse—more than once. Not to mention how unbelievable it is since you work in construction." She wiggled free of his body and headed toward the main-floor bathroom. "But if you want our hot, hulk of a neighbor to think you're a klutz instead of a stud, go for it."

Was that a clue? Derrick followed her, braced himself casually in the doorway and watched her freshen up. Once finished, she soaked a second washcloth with warm water, wrung it out and handed it to him. Always taking care of him. He was the luckiest man alive.

"You think the neighbor is hot?"

She rolled her eyes at his waggling eyebrows. "Well, duh."

Of course she thought the guy was hot. Tall, loaded with muscles and charming, the type all women drooled over. "Is that whose dick you were thinking about sucking?"

"No," deep-pink tinted her high cheekbones, "not him."

He caged her as she attempted to scoot by him. "Then who? Somebody I know?"

* * *

Heat rushed to Hanna's cheeks. She and Derrick had always had a fantastic sex life. Great communication, too. They talked about everything. No judgment, inside the bedroom or out. But telling him she thought the neighbor was hot and divulging the identity of the man whose cock she'd imagined sucking a few minutes ago were two different things. Doing so would push fantasy too close to reality.

"C'mon, baby. Tell me." The pads of Derrick's work-roughened fingertips grazed her cheek, tipped her chin upward. "Promise I won't be mad, no matter who it is."

Anybody could make that claim, but in Derrick's case, a promise was the real deal. Regardless of the topic, when he promised something, not only did he mean it, he stood by it without wavering. If she named her imaginary lover, Derrick was more likely to tease her than anything else. But the name would be out there.

"Remember that singer at The Pulse a couple weeks ago, the dark-haired one? Him." So she'd fibbed. No good could come of telling her husband she harbored lusty thoughts about his best friend. They had a very open relationship, but not *that* open.

"Yeah, I remember that guy." He dropped his hand from the wall to cup her breast and toy with her nipple—a soft, effortless touch that sent a new round of sparks through her system. "Was it his looks or the musician thing that turned you on?" The question might have been random interest, but the wheels turning behind Derrick's blue eyes hinted otherwise.

"Does it matter?"

"It might." A smile tugged at his sculpted lips—he had the 'I'm going to do bad things to you' look she'd fallen head-over-heels for a decade ago. "Get dressed so we can talk without me getting sidetracked again." A kiss on her forehead and he left her there, naked and a little confused.

"Talk about what?" she called after him, but he'd already disappeared from sight and, obviously, from earshot. She slipped into her silky robe and cinched the tie around her waist. Things were great between them. Solid as granite. Whatever he wanted to talk about, it couldn't be negative, right? The butterflies in her stomach didn't necessarily agree.

She hadn't kept him waiting long, yet he'd managed to sprawl out on the sectional. Due to the living room's furniture arrangement, and Derrick's love affair with the corner spot, he faced away as she approached. Not watching TV or playing on his cellphone, just waiting patiently, arms slung over the back of the sofa, legs stretched leisurely on the chaise portion. Comfortable. At ease. Good descriptions for Derrick in general, ninety-nine percent of the time.

When she hugged him from behind, he tipped his head back, making his sexy, chin-length blond hair rumple against the dark-brown cushions. "Hey, beautiful. Come around here and sit with me."

She did, happily settling between his parted thighs. But the butterflies remained, especially as she stared at two over-filled wine goblets on the coffee table. She'd never been much of a booze-hound. Even in her college years, she'd been a lightweight. She enjoyed having a cocktail at parties or a glass of wine with a nice dinner. But she didn't drink for the sake of drinking. It wasn't her thing and Derrick knew that. He never poured her a drink without asking. Well, almost never…

The scene in front of her had an uncomfortable familiarity. Three years had passed since that time, but looking at the glasses on the table took her right back to it. The day he'd given her the news about his vasectomy.

She'd known he didn't want kids when they got married. Not that he disliked them, but the abuse he'd suffered at the hands of his father had left its mark, deep down. He'd been upfront about his past and his future while they were dating. It had been a serious decision for her, because she'd always pictured herself having children. But her love for Derrick had won out.

That love hadn't prevented her from doing something stupid and selfish, though. Biology had kicked her maternal urges into high gear as she inched closer to thirty, and she'd secretly quit taking the Pill. She'd been sure he'd change his mind about having kids if she "accidentally" got pregnant. A bad idea. A lie that had almost destroyed her marriage.

After having one too many daiquiris at her twenty-eighth birthday party, she'd drunkenly confessed that she'd thrown the contraceptives away.

Derrick had been devastated by her deception. He'd explained to her—again—how terrified and certain he was that he'd turn out like his father if he had kids. God, the pain in his eyes when he voiced his fear of hurting those potential children. The look on his face when he'd realized that he couldn't even trust his own wife to help him prevent that from happening. He hadn't said the words outright, but she'd betrayed him.

Three weeks later, he'd set out two big glasses of wine, much like the ones on the table now, and told her he'd scheduled a vasectomy.

It'd been rough for a while after that. Worse than rough. There had been anger, disappointment, loss of trust. On both their parts. But when she'd searched her heart, what she wanted more than anything was a life with the man she loved. So she'd stayed. And thank god, Derrick had stayed too.

Counseling had helped. She had learned to take responsibility for her role in the disaster. No matter how badly she'd wanted a child, deceiving Derrick had not been okay. Their relationship had healed. More than that, it had grown stronger. Ninety percent of the time, she was blissfully happy. Not bad odds for any couple after spending a decade together. And if they could weather that storm, they could get through anything. Including whatever this talk meant.

"Want your drink?" Derrick asked, reaching around her for a glass.

"No, I really don't." The words came out harsher than she intended. "Sorry, it's just…the big glasses of wine and needing to talk to me about something, it reminds me of the past. Especially with my birthday on the horizon."

"Shit. I'm an ass. I didn't think."

"You know I love you and I'm happy with our life, but…it still hurts sometimes." She wasn't the perfect princess everybody pegged her for, her husband included. She made mistakes too.

"I know. I do. I'm sorry."

Tears welled in the corners of her eyes. "Stupid birthday. Stupid ovaries."

"Hey, ssshh…there is *nothing* about you that is stupid." He returned his glass to the table, untouched, then wrapped his arms around her and pulled her tight to his chest. "This isn't like that time. Nothing that'll make you sad or upset, I promise."

With that word, some of the tension slipped away. Derrick had never broken a promise to her. Including the one he'd made while they were dating, when he'd promised fatherhood would never be for him.

"Do you trust me?" His breath tickled her ear, making her shiver as she nodded. "Good. I need that right now, so I can tell you my idea. That's all it is, baby, an idea. If you say no, I won't mention it again."

"I don't know whether to be freaked out or excited." Though frankly, freaked out was in the lead. "Can you just tell me before my imagination runs away and joins the carnival?"

His deep chuckle caressed her soul as his hands did the same to her silk-covered breasts. "I want to take you to that little resort for your birthday. Make this birthday a celebration you'll never forget—for good reasons."

She tipped her head back and smiled at him. "Of course I'll say yes to that. Why wouldn't I?"

"Because you haven't heard the rest of it. I want to invite somebody to join us."

"Oh." Not what she'd imagined when she showed Derrick the private resort's website, but it'd still be fun. Maybe they could sneak out to the pool and skinny-dip in the moonlight, grab some alone time. "Well, I guess I can share you for a weekend."

A laugh burst from his mouth. He put his hard-earned muscles to use and shifted her to a straddle position that allowed her a view of his ruggedly handsome face.

She cupped his jaw, stroked the blond bristles of his goatee. "Whether we're alone or part of a group, I'll be with you, and that's all that matters. So, were you thinking of asking John and Tina? Tina and I can overload on treatments at the day-spa in town while you and John do the golf thing. Then, when I'm all prettied-up, you take me to the shops and buy me something ridiculously overpriced that I totally deserve."

"Baby, you don't need spa treatments to be gorgeous. And you deserve a hell of a lot more than I'll ever be able to give you – at home or in some fancy store."

And here came her guilt, galloping to the forefront. She'd made him feel like a loser. About the past. About being a tradesman instead of a polished professional with a six-figure income. "I didn't mean that the way it sounded. You know I don't care about money or things, and the rest…I'm at peace with, really."

"Yeah." One hand threaded through her hair, cupped the back of her head and drew her forward for a deep, soft kiss that ended way too quickly. "And your suggestions sound like a good time, but it's not what I had in mind. I meant we should invite one person to join us. A guy, and not so I have a golf buddy."

What? Oh god, his comment in the kitchen. He couldn't possibly mean it. Not seriously. "Then why invite a guy along?" She strung the words out, carefully and slowly, as if each one were a potential bomb.

"For you. I won't lie, though, it'd be for me too."

"Y-you want to be with a man?"

Derrick's sky-blue eyes bulged, and he shuddered. "No. Make that a giant *hell no*. It'd be for me because watching your body move and the expressions on your face, hearing the sexy sounds you make when you're getting off – those things turn me on more than anything in the world." Proof of his statement rubbed her through his shorts. "And I know the idea of being with two guys at once turns *you* on." At her nod, his eyes darkened. One hand slipped under the edge of her robe, his fingers walking up the inside of her thigh with deliberate slowness. "Only the truth between us, always, right?"

"Yes," she whispered, another pang of guilt stabbing at her for fibbing in the bathroom.

"If you're into it — and only if you're into it — I want to invite Jeremy to join us for a weekend at that resort."

"*You what?*" Oh god, oh god. Where was this coming from all of the sudden? Had he read her mind somehow, did she talk in her sleep — was it that obvious she was attracted to his best friend? She scrambled to get off his lap. Not happening. Derrick's strong hands kept her securely in place. One hand on her hip ensured her core remained pressed onto the hard ridge in his shorts. The other held her chin, gently yet firmly, forcing her to look into his eyes. So much passion there. So much love.

She swallowed dry air, only able to whisper when she finally spoke. "What did you have in mind?"

You around? Have time for a beer after work?

Jeremy tapped a reply while waiting for the red light to change. *Got back earlier today. When and where?*

Derrick's text popped up immediately. *Finishing up on a site. Thirty minutes. JT's Roadhouse?*

Sounds good. See you there. The car behind him honked as he hit send. Jeremy flipped his middle finger at the rearview mirror, chuckling as the attractive woman in the sporty coupe behind him returned the gesture through her front window — while smiling. Playful, then, not bitchy.

All right. If he hadn't just committed to meeting his buddy, he'd engage the cute redhead in some more eye contact and see if he could get her out of that car and into his bed. He honked and hit the accelerator. Another time, with another woman.

Pretty rare thing, hearing from Derrick during the week. He and Derrick had always been close, remaining tight through the years despite their very different lives. While much of Jeremy's time went to commuting, jetting across the country and around the globe on business, Derrick usually spent his non-work hours close to home with his wife. Maybe Hanna had plans and Derrick was grabbing the opportunity to hang. Or maybe shit was brewing. His friend's marriage seemed impenetrable, but looks could be deceiving. Nobody knew that better than him.

The Hummer's steering wheel squeaked under his clenched fists. He'd signed away his wife and day-to-day life with his son almost a year ago. Fucking bullshit, that. He still didn't understand exactly what'd gone wrong. Probably never would.

He pulled into his driveway faster than necessary, just for the jolt of slamming on the brakes. Thinking about Viv always stirred him up. Some ways good, others not so much. He'd loved her, worked his ass off to give their family the best of the best, been one hundred percent faithful despite the blanket of frost she'd thrown over their bed—and it hadn't been enough. Fuck that shit. He wouldn't wish the stabbed-in-the-heart feeling on anybody.

Inside the house, he ditched his suit for jeans and a tee. He did a half-assed job of making the bed, then checked the nightstand drawer. Two condoms left, enough should he happen to meet somebody later. Sex, not love. All he needed from here out.

Jeremy spotted Derrick's motorcycle the second he pulled into the parking lot. His buddy hadn't wasted any time getting here. Jeremy found a spot, then headed toward the front door.

"Hey, Jer, over here." Derrick's voice and extended arm stopped Jeremy before he reached the building. "Patio okay with you?" he asked as Jeremy cut around some empty tables.

He dropped into one of the dark-green, plastic chairs. "Sure, I'm easy."

"That's an understatement."

"True. Jealous?"

Derrick grinned. "Nope. Not in the slightest."

"Bullshit."

"No B.S." Derrick tipped a bottle of Coors Light to his lips and drained its contents. He pushed the empty aside and signaled the waitress for two more, then slid his cell phone across the table. "Not when I have this waiting for me every single day."

"Holy shit." Jeremy knew he should look away, that Derrick probably meant to show him a picture of Hanna in a dress or maybe a bikini, but he couldn't tear his eyes from the phone. Hanna looked up at him from the screen, a sex-kitten smile on her lips as she peeked over her shoulder. But it wasn't only her pretty face holding him captive. Hell no.

Her ass was front and center, a tiny pink thong barely covering the essentials as she posed doggy-style for the camera—and her husband. "She's gorgeous, but I think you pulled up the wrong picture." Mercifully, the phone disappeared into Derrick's palm. "Sorry for staring."

"S'okay. And you're right," Derrick double-checked the display before handing it over again, "I meant to show you this one."

"Christ, D, how many beers have you had?" His buddy had to be half-tanked to be showing him this—Hanna, on her knees, wearing nothing but those same pink panties, her red-painted fingertips covering little more than the nipples of her incredible rack. The shot put most centerfold pics to shame. Maybe because of the genuine emotion in her eyes and smile. Maybe because he knew her, how great she was in real life. Either way, fuck.

"Just that one Coors. Totally sober over here." Derrick's reply yanked Jeremy's attention from the photo he should *not* be looking at.

Silently finding your best buddy's wife hot was one thing, ogling naked pictures of her—courtesy of her husband—that was goddamn surreal.

Jeremy turned the phone facedown as their server arrived with two bottles of beer. "I got this." He pulled his wallet from his jeans and paid the waitress, then pushed the phone toward its rightful owner. Alcohol wasn't really his thing, but he took a long pull anyway, buying time.

Derrick matched the pace with his beer, his eyes never leaving Jeremy's face. Gauging him? Something was going on. Hell if Jeremy knew what it was, though.

Derrick drank and waited. Even grinned a little. But say something that'd explain what'd just happened? No. Only, "You look sort of freaked out."

"You showed me naked pictures of your wife, man."

"And what'd you think?"

"I think you're lucky I'm not going to tell Hanna about your moment of temporary insanity, or she'd have your nuts on the chopping block." He pushed his half-full bottle to the middle of the table and leaned back in his chair. "Want to tell me what the fuck is going on with you? Everything okay on the home front?"

"Yeah, nothing new or bad to report." Derek polished off the rest of his beer. Instead of motioning for the waitress, he twirled the empty bottle on the table. "But there is something I want to talk to you about."

"Sure."

"I want to give Hanna something. Something I know she's wanted for a long time."

"Yeah? Good for you guys." He reached over and issued a congratulatory punch to the shoulder. "You're going to love it, you know. Nothing better in the world."

Derrick's eyes narrowed. He even waved off the waitress.

"You weren't talking about giving your wife a baby."

"No."

Well, shit. "Sorry, man."

"Don't be. I know you love the being-a-dad thing and Luke is a great kid. I like being his honorary uncle, but I can't do more than that. You know where I came from, how I'd wind up treating a kid of my own."

No point in rehashing that argument again. Jeremy had tried repeatedly, but no amount of talking had convinced Derrick he could break the Sutter family mold. Too bad. Derrick would make a great dad, whether he believed it or not.

Jeremy settled against the patio chair, using its hard plastic ribs to scratch a spot in the middle of his back. "So what's the thing—diamonds, a trip to Europe, a puppy?"

"A threesome."

If he'd had anything in his mouth, it'd be two tables over now. "Fuck off. Seriously?"

"Seriously." Derrick's index finger tapped the back of his phone where it rested on the table. *Tap, tap, tap. Tap, tap, tap.*

The pictures. Derrick wanting to talk to him about something. No fucking way. "Holy shit. You're asking *me*, aren't you?" And there it was, the nod. "You need to give this some serious thought, D. About a year's worth, minimum. Don't jump in dick first, use your brain. Your heart."

"I have. I am. Things are great between us, but sometimes she gets this faraway look in her eyes, especially around her birthday. I don't have to ask, I know what it's about, but that's off the table. This is for her, Jer. To make her other fantasy come true. If it'll make her happy, I want to give it to her, you know?"

Yeah, he got that. He'd tried giving Viv everything—fancy house, money in the bank, a family—she'd left anyway. Life and love didn't come with guarantees, and this plan of Derrick's could blow up spectacularly. Jeremy would be a shitty friend if he didn't point that out, no matter how much his cock liked the idea of getting naked with Hanna.

"Counseling might be a better option than a ménage."

Derrick barked out a single laugh. "We took the therapy route three years ago. We're good. I know it in my gut. She could've left me back then but she didn't, and thank fucking god for that because I can't imagine my life without her in it."

"Let's roll with that theme. Say you do this threesome thing. You really think that when the moment comes, pardon the pun, you'll be okay letting somebody else touch Hanna? Watching your wife get wild with another guy? Because once it's done, it's done, no going back. It could fuck up your relationship permanently."

"It won't. Not if you're the third."

"I'm not sure if that's a credit to my loyalty or an insult to my masculinity." The insanity of it all made him laugh hard enough to draw attention from a pair of good-looking women a couple tables over. He snagged his beer, saluted, and took a swig. "You and Hanna have discussed all the details, including the part where I'm the one walking into your bedroom?"

"Yeah," a massive grin slid into place, "several times."

"Shit, I've seen that look before." And envied it. His buddy had scored big-time on that long-ago night. If Jeremy had won the coin toss in the bar a decade ago, they wouldn't be having this fucked-up conversation. Because if he'd won the chance to hit on Hanna, if he'd been the one to land her, he sure as hell wouldn't share her.

"Well?" A couple of swipes and taps later, Derrick pushed his cell across the table. "What should I tell her?"

Looking was a mistake, yet the phone was in his hand, inches from his face. He should've known it'd be another explicit picture. Okay, truth—he'd hoped it would be. But this—Christ.

"Go ahead, play it."

A video. Of Hanna. What was one more mistake? He tapped the arrow in the center of the screen. The clip started innocently enough. As innocent as it could be with Hanna wearing only those pink panties. She wasn't covering her tits this time and they were goddamn spectacular. His mouth literally watered at the sight of them. She waved and giggled, managing to look beautiful, sexy and sweet all at once. His best friend's *wife*, for crying out loud. Something he needed to remember.

"Hi, Jeremy." Her soft voice drifted through the phone's speaker. "I hope we'll um...see you soon." Another giggle, then the video stopped. A personal invitation. For him.

Reluctantly, he passed the phone back. "Tell her I'll be there."

Chapter Three

"I can't believe you're going through with this. No, scratch that. I can't believe *Derrick* is going through with this."

"I know, it's wild." Hanna rolled her little red dress to prevent it from creasing. She tucked it into her suitcase while smiling at her bestie, who'd parked herself in the center of the bed to oversee the activity. "When I tried to, um, jump him this morning, he told me I had to wait until we *all* got to the resort later."

Megan's jaw dropped. "Holy shitballs, he's for-real making this happen. A threesome for your birthday. Wonder what he'll give you next year?" She laughed while ducking the pillow Hanna launched at her head, then picked up a pair of panties from the to-be-packed pile. "And speaking of holy shitballs..." Megan gaped at the panties — sheer black lace in the front, a web of ribbons in the back and not much in between. "These would drive any man crazy."

"I hope so," Hanna said, scooping them from her friend's hand.

"Ready to tell me who the other guy is?"

"Can't, sorry. Part of the agreement." A fat load of hooey, but necessary. Megan's interrogation next week would be thorough enough. If her friend knew the extra man in this adventure was Jeremy Cruz, Derrick's best friend since forever, she'd never give Hanna a moment's peace.

"But he's hot, right?"

An image of Jeremy popped into Hanna's head. She smiled at Megan, so wide it almost hurt her face. "Very hot."

"You're mean."

"I know."

"And the luckiest woman alive."

"I know that too."

"It's totally unfair." Megan dropped onto her stomach, head resting on her hands. "Your husband is this badass-looking super-hunk who worships the ground you walk on, and now you're getting a second hottie to play with? I'd call you a bitch if you weren't so freaking nice."

"Gee, thanks."

"You're welcome...bitch." Megan giggled. "Sorry, had to."

"Just for that, I'm not showing you what's in here." Hanna waved a black, cinch-topped bag.

"Sex toys?"

"Yup."

"You really are cruel." Megan laughed, then stuck out her tongue. "Seriously, take pity on the chronically undersexed here and show me the goods."

"Pfft. If you're not getting any, it's by choice and we both know it. And there's nothing crazy in here." She dropped the bag into the suitcase. "Just your standard-issue vibrators and stuff, nothing too kinky." By her standards, anyway.

"But you'll be with *two men* when you use them. I call that damn kinky." Megan sighed as Hanna zipped up the case. "At least tell me what the second guy looks like. Throw me a crumb, for god's sake."

As if her friend needed a crumb. In her position as ECE in Hanna's kindergarten classroom, Megan turned every man's head when she opened the door in the mornings, especially the single dads. Many of them had sent Christmas and end-of-the-year gifts for *Miss* Atherton last year—and those gifts often included phone numbers. Unfortunately for the men, Megan refused to date anybody she'd be forced to see post-hookup. Too awkward.

Hanna hoped to god that wouldn't be the case with Jeremy after this weekend. Aside from secretly fantasizing about the man for years, she'd always liked him. Enjoyed his presence when he hung out with Derrick. Jeremy was as fun and nice as he was attractive. Despite his job as a bigwig consultant and the barrage of expensive toys it afforded him, he was totally down to earth. It came through in his easygoing laugh and the pure love he emanated when he talked about Luke, his four-year-old son. Simply put, the man was a catch. Or would be, if he hadn't sworn off relationships after the Vivien mess.

"Earth to Hanna…"

And she'd totally been caught daydreaming.

"Spill it, chickie. Description."

"Oh fine." She rolled her eyes at Megan, who was currently rubbing her hands together as if she were about to get some amazing scoop. "He's a bit over six feet with short, dark hair. A strong nose—"

"Wait. Is that a nice way of saying he has a big honker?"

"It's not *that* big."

Megan's eyebrows rose. "I hope you won't be saying the same thing about his cock a few hours from now."

"Oh my god, you're horrible." Yet Hanna couldn't help laughing. Leave it to Megan to get to the *meat* of the matter.

"But I bring up a valid point, right? He could be wind up being a disappointment in the groinal region, unless…you've already seen it, maybe in a picture?"

"I haven't. But I'm not worried."

"Yeah, I guess it doesn't really matter, since you won't be fucking him."

"Right." Better to leave it at that than tell Megan that Derrick had seen the other guy naked, many times. That'd raise too many questions.

"Okay, so he has a big nose but he's no Cyrano de Bergerac. What else?"

"Clean-shaven with a manly jaw, twinkling brown eyes, charming smile and the whitest teeth I've ever seen on a real person." Yikes, maybe that was a bit too much detail. And enthusiasm.

"Oh. My. God." Megan hopped off the bed, grabbed Hanna by the shoulders and stared at her with enormous eyes. "It's Jeremy fucking Cruz!"

Oh god—busted. Busted hard. "Why would you think that?" she asked, her attempt at innocent surprise totally ruined by the hot blush currently staining her cheeks.

"Because I know you—and Derrick, for that matter—well enough to know neither of you would invite a total stranger along for something this intimate. I just thought it might've been somebody he knew from work. This is even better. Jeremy is hot, hot, wowza-freakin' hot."

Hanna groaned again. She squeezed her eyes closed, but when she opened them, Megan's face was still right there, sporting a giddy, teenage-girlish grin.

God help her next week—Megan was going to want a minute-by-minute, lick-by-lick account of the weekend's activities.

"Well, girlfriend..." Megan released her and flopped on the bed, winking as she patted Hanna's suitcase. "Seems like you're ready for tonight."

With that comment, the nerves set in for the hundredth time. "I'm not sure I am, to be honest." In her various conversations with Megan about Derrick's proposition, she'd kept the focus on the sex, not her insecurities. Kind of late to be laying them out now, but she had to. "I still don't get it, why Derrick wants to do this, how he's okay with it. He's never been an overly jealous guy, but this takes that to the extreme."

"What does he say when you ask him?"

"That he wants to make me happy." Her voice tapered off at the end, and no amount of throat-clearing brought moisture into her dry mouth. The rest came out as a scratchy whisper. "Make my dreams come true." Stupid tears. Especially the one sliding down her cheek. "Crap."

"Oh, honey. Come here..." Megan's arms folded around her. "You should talk to him again. It's been three years, maybe he'd consider a reversal."

Megan was her best friend and they shared a lot of personal stuff. Hanna had told her that Derrick came from an abusive home. But she'd never divulged the horrifying details—the dark demons that prevented him from trusting himself. She couldn't expect Megan to understand without that information. Even with it, it had taken Hanna years—and a huge mistake—to fully comprehend the depth of his fear.

She broke free of Megan's embrace and wiped her cheeks. "Honestly, I'm fine. The birthday thing always messes me up. It's like PMS, multiplied by twelve."

"Good god." Megan shuddered. "You're sure you're okay?"

"I am." Hanna offered one hand, four of its five fingers balled together, the smallest one extended and wiggling. "I pinky swear it."

An *hmph* slipped from Megan's mouth as she curled her pinky finger around Hanna's. "Then back to the question of 'why'. Could Derrick be testing you? And don't hate *me* for going this route—what about compensating for a guilty conscience?"

"No and no, I'm sure of it." Which only left one thing, the reason he'd told her over and over. "He's doing it for me."

"I think you're right." Megan's eyes drifted to the suitcase, then back to Hanna's face. "I guess you'd better decide if you're going to let him."

When Derrick's buddy agreed to the threesome, it'd been with one condition—a waiting period. A few weeks for his best friend to wrap up some out-of-town project he had going, plus get a clean bill of health from the doc. Those were the reasons Jer had verbalized. Legit for sure, and good ones, but Derrick bet Jeremy had an ulterior motive, like giving them time to change their minds.

They hadn't. Over the course of the month, Derrick had had the hottest sex of his life with his wife, and he knew without asking that she'd agree with that assessment. Every time they'd discussed details for the trip to Havenbrook Resort, Hanna had gotten so turned on she'd been practically insatiable. Hopefully Jeremy had gotten some rest this week — or packed some Viagra.

"This is it." Derrick grinned at the best thing ever to happen to him as he pulled into a spot in front of the large, stone building that housed the resort's offices and intimate restaurant. "Time to check in and get your birthday party started." He leaned over for a kiss that landed on hesitant lips, rather than hungry ones. Not good. Neither was the glassiness in her beautiful eyes. "Hey, what's this, why the tears?"

There'd been no sign of trouble earlier. They'd made the two-hour drive with the top down on her convertible Beetle, Hanna laughing at the wind whipping her hair, both of them talking about music, movies and other casual stuff.

He brushed away the single, fat drop that'd rolled down her cheek. Cupped her face between his palms. "This weekend is about you. We can change the plans, postpone them, call the whole thing off permanently, anything you want. Talk to me."

"Now that we're here and it's almost real, I'm scared."

"Of what, baby?"

"Things changing between us." Her hands closed around his wrists and squeezed. "What if you're not okay with it, once it's happening, or afterward? I can't lose you."

"That'll never happen. I love you. You won't lose me, I promise."

"That's easy to say now," she whispered.

Hurting her, even a little, was the absolute last thing he wanted to do. "I'm going to call Jer," he grabbed his cell from the cup holder, "tell him we'd like to be on our own this weekend. A romantic weekend, just the two of us. We can decide whether to try this again later."

Her lips parted as if to speak, then her head jerked sideways at the sound of a horn.

Jeremy. His black Hummer rolled up, filling the neighboring spot. He leaned out the open window and smiled down at them, at Hanna in particular. "You guys check in already?"

Shit. "Not yet. Give us a couple minutes here."

"Yeah, of course," Jeremy said, pulling his arm and head back inside his vehicle until Hanna's voice stopped him.

"Wait—it's okay, Jeremy, we're ready."

No hesitation or wavering in her voice now, but Derrick wasn't taking this thing one step further until he was sure. "I meant what I said, baby. We only do this if you want to."

Hanna glanced at Jeremy's face in the Hummer's window, then back to him. "Only if we *both* want to." His wink must've been reassurance enough, because a new smile lit her face, beginning on her kissable lips and spreading to her shining eyes. "Okay."

"Yeah?"

"Yes. I love you. I trust you."

"Good." This time when he kissed her, she melted into it. Opening for him, letting him tip her head back and plunder her mouth while palming one breast through her t-shirt, for Jeremy and the rest of the world to see. She moaned against his lips, Jeremy's wolf-whistle sounded from above them, and blood raced to Derrick's cock. "Good" didn't begin to describe the plans he had for the weekend.

"Take your time." Derrick's lips grazed hers, pulling away exactly when she wanted him to give her more.

"Tease."

"You like it that way—it makes you hot. Speaking of hot...damn, baby, that suit." He winked, grabbed a towel and headed across the room. "We'll see you at the pool."

Then he was gone. Beyond the closed door, his voice and laugh mingled with Jeremy's before fading away. And for the third time today, the reality of what—and who—was to come slammed into her brain.

"Oh god." She dropped onto the king-size bed. Wrong move, it only made the thoughts rush in faster. Thoughts of what would happen on this bed a few hours from now. Dirty, delicious things involving two gorgeous men and immense amounts of pleasure. Because her husband wanted to bring her hottest fantasy to life. With Jeremy. And that's what made this weekend an even wilder ride.

Ten years ago, she'd been out for a girls' night. Lots of drinking on her friends' parts, mostly dancing on hers. Maybe a hook-up, if somebody caught her eye. Two guys had. Buddies, obviously—both of them handsome and built, each had asked her to dance throughout the evening.

Even way back then, when the most adventurous thing she'd done was have orgasmless intercourse at a drive-in movie, the thought of being sexually sandwiched between Derrick and Jeremy had been front and center in her thoughts. If they'd asked her to go home with them—with *both* of them—that night, she would have. At last call, Jeremy had kissed her cheek and said good night. Derrick's kiss had been less gentlemanly. There'd been no "goodnight" from him, but it'd definitely been a good night. The beginning of a long-lasting relationship with an incredible man.

She'd never looked back and wondered what-if about Jeremy, but she couldn't deny that she'd continued looking *at* him. Imagining him as guy-number-two when she and Derrick role-played. She'd replaced him with other imaginary, faceless men for the duration of his marriage to Vivien—it would've been too weird to sit and talk with her, otherwise—but when Vivien had been crazy enough to divorce him, Hanna had welcomed Jeremy back to her fantasies. Immediately.

While she'd never actually told Derrick about her ongoing attraction to his best friend, he'd obviously figured it out. According to Derrick, though, he had another reason for choosing Jeremy this weekend. Trust. He trusted Jeremy's discretion. He trusted his friend to respect the rules they'd laid out. He trusted the man not to try and steal his wife.

Most importantly, though, he trusted her.

Time she accepted her husband's gift. She rolled off the bed and padded across the plush carpeting to the dresser for a look in the mirror. She turned side to side. The red swimsuit was sexy. Pretty too. It showed off her cleavage, which probably factored into Derrick's approval. But it didn't pack the punch of the other suit she'd bought. A little digging and she came up with the white one.

Made of crocheted fabric over skin-colored lining, this bikini gave the illusion of being see-through. Now *this* would have Derrick falling all over himself to touch her. That's the reaction she wanted—from two men.

She tucked her room key, sunscreen and towel into a shoulder bag. *Go time.*

Around the exclusive adults-only resort, elaborately carved signposts directed guests to their destination. The main building. Each of the half a dozen, interspersed, individually named cabins. And her current target—the pool. Beautifully manicured gardens lined the cobblestone path, scenting the July air. Birds chirped in the surrounding greenery, their songs the sole sound in her ears until she reached the black iron fence enclosing the pool area. Familiar male voices and laughter joined the mix. Until she pushed through the gate.

She'd hoped for a whistle, maybe a compliment from her always appreciative husband. The complete silence and gaping mouths on Derrick and Jeremy were ten times better. Nothing like a couple of drooling hunks to make a girl feel sexy.

"I can't believe we have the pool to ourselves when it's so gorgeous out here." Thank god she'd worn flat sandals, there's no way she'd have balanced on heels right now. "Lucky us."

"Exactly what I was thinking," Jeremy said. He rose from a lounge chair to relieve her of her bag. The act brought his fingers into contact with her shoulder. Fingers that made themselves at home on her skin as they trailed lazily down her arm.

Now *her* bottom lip fell. She could probably shoot sparks from her fingertips with the jolt of electricity his simple touch had caused. She'd expected him to join in later, not make the first move.

"You can thank Jer for the privacy. He threw some cash at the older couple who were here so they'd take off." Derrick's words slid into her ear from behind. And on the subject of behinds, his rather solid cock now pressed against hers.

With Derrick behind her, she had nowhere to look but straight ahead, at Jeremy. "You paid people to leave, really?" Wow, that was so…ballsy. Take charge. And totally hot. Thank god for the lining in her swimsuit, because pointing was rude and her nipples were definitely aiming at him. "Thank you."

"Very polite, baby, but you can thank him better than that." With a single step, Derrick moved her closer to Jeremy. Definitely within sandwich range.

"H-how should I thank him?"

"Any way he wants."

She shivered at Derrick's answer, or maybe at Jeremy's sinful lips smiling down at her. "Here, n-now? Somebody might come along and catch us."

"Odds of that are pretty good." Jeremy caught her hands and pulled her away from the safety of Derrick's body, past the lounge chairs, to the edge of the pool. "Since we'll be swimming." Without further warning, he dove in, his very fine body slicing the surface without spraying a single drop of water in her direction.

"How is it—warm?" she asked when he resurfaced.

He slid a hand over his dark hair. Smiled at her so devilishly, she really should have clued in that something was up.

"Let's find out." In a heartbeat, Derrick scooped her into his arms, took a couple of running steps, drew up his knees and cannonballed them both into the deep end.

Water rushed into her ears, creating that distinctive sound that comes from plummeting beneath the surface, no holds barred. The way Derrick did everything. The way he made her do things — taking a risk, always enjoying the ride. Like this weekend. Like this moment.

She opened her eyes underwater. Derrick was right there, little bubbles rising from his wide-mouthed grin. God, she loved him. She reached for him and he towed her in, hugged her tight to his chest, then kicked his legs and took them up. As soon as their heads broke the surface, his mouth covered hers. His tongue demanded entry, control. He could have it. She wanted him to have it.

She twined her arms at the back of his neck, did the same with her legs around his waist. Small waves lapped at her as he moved them to shallower water. She knew the second he had a solid footing, because he found her bikini bottom and slid a hand beneath the flimsy fabric.

"Nice ass." He breathed the words against her lips between kisses. "I'm going to fuck it while you suck Jer's cock. Nice and deep, both of us. My dick right here, buried inside you," one finger pressed teasingly on target, "while Jer's is down your throat."

Oh god. She tried to hold back, but it was futile, the moan escaped. No point in trying to resist him. Them. Even the *idea* of them made her desperate. She surrendered to her need and ground against the hard-on in his swim trunks.

"You can't wait, can you, baby?" He chuckled at the admission her shaking head represented. "Don't worry, we'll give you something to tide you over until after dinner, won't we, Jer?"

"Oh yeah." Jeremy's big, hard body connected with her back. He skimmed his hands over her arms, her shoulders. He closed his fist around the drenched hair at her nape and tucked it to one side. Hot breath tickled her damp skin. Then lips. Jeremy's lips — on her neck.

She closed her eyes. Gave in to it. The sensations. The reality of two incredible men touching and kissing her at the same time.

Jeremy's hands glided around front, separating her from Derrick enough to slide down, into the front of her bikini. His low rumble filled her ear as his fingers added more exquisite, teasing pressure to her clit. "Forget hitting the restaurant later, I've got my appetizer right here."

"You have no idea, Jer. Wait 'til you taste her."

Her eyes snapped open. With his water-slicked blond hair, killer dimples and just-rough-enough goatee, Derrick was lethally sexy. Any woman's fantasy, and he belonged to her, only her. She would never share him, yet he was doing this for her. She should stop this before it went any further.

"Maybe I should have a sample right now. What do you think, D?"

She shook her head, tried hugging Derrick tighter. All this earned her was another sexy chuckle from her husband. He probably mistook her clinginess as play, not panic. She held fast, kissed him until he broke it, a glint in his eye as he extricated himself from her slippery arms and legs.

"You definitely should," he stepped back, "but I guarantee a sample won't cut it."

"Then I'll keep going until I've had enough." Jeremy's arm clamped around her waist before she could respond. "Or until Hanna can't take any more."

"Good luck with that, Jer. She's insatiable."

Oh god, Derrick had just given Jeremy permission—no, encouragement—to give her oral. Here. Now. She'd expected a playful afternoon, not that they'd dive right in to the hot stuff.

"You look gorgeous in this bathing suit, Hanna. But I know you're going to look even better out of it."

"Thank you." A ridiculous answer to Jeremy's sexy compliments, but she couldn't turn off the Miss Manners thing, ever. It was too deeply engrained.

"No, thank you. I haven't stopped thinking about your video invitation all month—it gave me something to focus on, especially late at night." Jeremy's lips grazed the shell of her ear, his deep, smooth voice filling her head and sending a string of sparks zinging through her body.

She rolled her hips and he tightened his hold, pressing a very solid erection against her ass. Whatever she *should* have done might as well have sunk to the bottom of the deep end. She wanted this. Wanted Jeremy's mouth between her legs, his cock sliding between her lips, down her throat. So much she was salivating.

He lifted her from the water and perched her on the edge of the pool. A short row of white lounge chairs formed a line behind her. With the tall, iron fence and landscaping, the pool area offered a fair amount of privacy. Good thing, since he'd positioned himself between her legs, and his thumb was brushing back and forth over her bikini-covered clit.

From a dozen feet away, Derrick watched. His eyes stayed locked with hers, intense, even from this distance. Did he want her to stop, move away from Jeremy? Why didn't he call to her, rush over and stake sole claim? She stared. Pleaded with her eyes. He didn't budge. Gave nothing away.

Jeremy's lips found her neck again, licking and kissing as his fingers slipped inside her bikini bottoms. "So hot. I know I'm supposed to tease you, but I want to make you come. Right now." He increased the pressure, and her hips rocked forward of their own volition.

She fought to keep her eyes open, to focus on her husband. But dear god, Jeremy's hand... Her eyelids fluttered closed. *Make good choices*, her mantra, five days a week for ten months of the year, rang in her head. *Tell Jeremy to stop, end this.* She didn't. A moan escaped her lips, loud against the thick silence of the moment.

The sound of Derrick diving beneath the surface was louder.

Her eyes snapped open, but he'd disappeared from her line of sight. "Derrick..."

"Hanna." Jeremy's free hand moved to her face. He cupped her chin, a subtle demand for eye contact. "He's good. Stop worrying and trust us."

"Listen to the man, he's right." Derrick stepped into her peripheral vision, totally sexy with his dripping, chin-length hair, his strong hands swiping beads of water from those toned, fully inked arms. He settled behind her, his chest pressed to her back, bracketing her legs with his thighs. His mustache and beard rasped her neck, a contrast from Jeremy's clean-shaven skin. So different, these men. Derrick's hands slid inside her bikini top. "You cold, baby?"

She shook her head, speechless. Impossible to form words while sandwiched between them, Derrick teasing her nipples and Jeremy's hand working magic inside her bikini bottoms.

"Then you must be all kinds of hot, because these gems," a tug on the skimpy fabric bared her breasts completely, "are hard enough to cut glass." He scooped one breast into his palm. "And perfect for sucking. Don't you think, Jer?"

No air, she had no air. Her pulse pounded in her temples. As if in slow motion, Jeremy's dark head lowered to her breast. Warm lips covered her nipple. His swirling tongue gave way to scraping teeth.

Derrick's work-roughened fingertips caressed her other breast. Soft touches that ended with firm tugging on her nipple. Her neck received a similar assault— light kisses mixed with the burn created by the unyielding clamp of his teeth.

"Make me come," she whispered. "Please."

"You heard the lady." Derrick curled his hand around the edge of her bikini bottom and pulled it aside, giving Jeremy better access. "Time you had that taste."

"With pleasure." Jeremy worked his way down, kissing a trail that led straight to her clit.

Oh god. And there went her pulse, as high as the sun beating down on the three of them.

"I've got you, baby." Her husband's calloused hands warmed her breasts. His breath tickled her ear as his low, gravelly voice filled her head. "Lean on me and let go. Enjoy."

"Derrick, I—" Words gone. Good intentions gone. She pushed her fingers through Jeremy's hair and clutched him tighter. So close, right there, on the edge...

"Yeah, like that. Grind against his face." Derrick's hard pinches sent streaks of electricity from her nipples to her clit. "So fucking hot when you come — let me see it."

"Yes, that..." The first wave rushed over her. Jeremy's arms settled on her shaking legs, holding her in place as he drove her to the peak, then beyond, through another spiral of blinding sensation. She grabbed Derrick's biceps, dug her nails in. Panted and moaned as her head fell back against his chest.

"Slide into the pool," Derrick said near her ear. "I'm right behind you."

Obeying him was automatic. Always. She nodded and eased off the concrete edge, into water that felt much cooler than the first time around.

Derrick's body entered the water with a pronounced splash, and then he was behind her, as promised. "Good thing you're easy." Choked laughter sputtered from him as she landed an elbow to his solar plexus. He righted her bikini top and turned her toward the gate. "'Cause we have company."

"Oh shit." Her shocked curse earned a laugh from both men.

"I love it when the kindergarten teacher swears." Derrick pulled her into his arms. "Very hot."

"You think everything is hot."

He squeezed her tight. "Everything about *you*, fucking right."

A moony-eyed, twenty-something couple closed the gate. They wandered, arms wrapped around each other, to a pair of lounge chairs at the end of the pool.

"Did they see...anything?"

"Nothing. We heard them while they were still on the path." Derrick rubbed his beard against her neck, a gesture of possession and affection that made her heart skip a beat every time he did it. "I promised we'd take care of you, baby."

They'd certainly done that. On several levels, the memory of which had heat rushing to her cheeks — and between her legs.

"But unfortunately, I had to quit before I made good on my word." A few feet in front of her, Jeremy treaded water, his face sporting one of his uber-charming smiles. "To sample you until you couldn't take any more."

Oh god.

"Guess I'll have to try again later," he said, winking as he dove beneath the water and swam away. He resurfaced across the pool, climbed out, wrapped a towel around his waist and left through the gate without a single look back.

"Is he—" No, anything about Jeremy was the wrong question. She turned in Derrick's arms but kept her eyes downcast. Another man had just gotten her off in front of him. How could she look him in the eye after that? "Are we okay?"

He caught her chin and tipped it up. "Yeah, baby, we're more than okay." A wicked smile pulled his lips into a sexy curve. "But I need to fuck you."

"I need that too. Let's go."

The slow shake of his head told her his intentions before he spoke another word. "Can't wait. Need to be inside my wife. Right now."

The ownership in his words, in the tone of his voice and his hands on her body, gave her goose bumps. He'd shared her with Jeremy for her pleasure, but there was no mistaking who she truly belonged to, body and soul.

Her back bumped the wall of the pool. Water lapped at the swell of her breasts. Between them, Derrick pushed his trunks down enough to free his cock. It pressed against her belly as he pulled the bikini bottoms to one side, as he'd done for Jeremy. His crystal-blue eyes darkened with lust and intent. This time was all about him.

His knuckles brushed her hip as he fisted his cock and directed it between her thighs. "Wrap your legs around me." He tipped his head to block her view as she glanced over his shoulder at the couple. "Forget about them, eyes on me."

Her pulse beat hard against her temples, Derrick's demand amplifying the effect. She locked her arms behind his neck and hoisted her legs into place around his waist. The head of his cock nudged her entrance. Right now it would appear they were hugging. Once Derrick was inside her, fucking her, there'd be no mistaking their act. There'd be waves. And even if *she* stayed silent, Derrick rarely did.

They would get caught.

"That is one naughty smile."

"Is it?" she asked in her sweetest, kindergarten-teacher voice.

"Oh yeah." His chuckle rumbled between them, his warm breath tickling her lips.

She threaded her fingers through his hair where it hung behind his ears. "Mmm, you're right. I need my husband inside me, fucking me, right now."

* * *

And that's what she'd get. A slight shift and Derrick had her exactly where he wanted her. He tightened his grip on her hips, dug his fingers in enough to make her gasp. Yeah, there'd be marks later. His beauty bruised easily and he usually took care how he handled her, but not this time. He had to make sure she knew.

"You're mine." He pulled her down hard, groaning between gritted teeth as she took him in.

"Always and only."

He maintained his tight hold, pulled back and thrust again, fast and balls-deep, forcing another sharp gasp from her lips. "Too hard, baby?"

"No, I want it this way." She tugged him by the hair until their foreheads touched and no visible space remained between them. "Kiss me, fuck me, hard and fast, all of it. I need you to."

Proof that she was his and his alone, he got that. He sealed their lips together, pushed his tongue into her mouth. Her taste — not some artificial mint or fruit, just this delicious, indescribable thing that was one-hundred-percent, pure *Hanna* — worked its way through him. Starting on the tip of his tongue, it filled his head, spread through his body like a sweet-hot streak that made every inch of him more alive than any adrenaline rush. As it had since their first kiss.

He thrust. Deep. Hard. Water slapped against his back, his arms. He swallowed Hanna's moans as he pushed inside, again and again. Sparks of pain shot out where his knuckles ground against the concrete pool wall. More where Hanna's nails dug into his scalp.

"Do it," she whispered between the smacking of lips and clashing teeth. "Come."

Magic fucking words. Fire licked at the base of his cock, raced up his shaft. One final push buried him deep in heaven, and he let go, coming like a fucking teenager until everything from the nuts down went numb and he had to lean on her to stay upright.

"Jesus."

Her warm, hitched breathing filled his ear, his head. Then she regained her voice, and apparently, her wit. "I'm pretty sure Jesus has left the pool area."

He laughed. Rubbed his beard against her neck, smiling when she tilted to give him better access. "What about the honeymooners — they leave too?"

"Oh, I'm allowed to look at them now?" She wiggled, separating them below the waist and regaining her footing. A quick peek over his shoulder and she whispered, "Oh my god, I don't believe it — they're still sitting there."

"Don't worry, baby, I don't think you gave us away."

"*Me?*"

He half-winced, half-laughed at the hard pinch her normally gentle hand administered to his waist. "Shit, that's deadly. You have a license for that thing?"

"Yes, and I'm putting it back in your trunks." Beneath the surface, she snapped the elastic against his abdomen. The most amazing eyes in the world looked into his, full of love and amusement.

If he could've dropped to his knees right then, he would have. "I would die for you, baby."

"How about you get me out of here in a way that doesn't scream 'we just had sex in the pool' instead?"

"You got it." In a move that elicited on of his favorite sounds — Hanna shrieking — he switched them around, so her body draped over his, piggyback style.

He carried her across the pool and up the steps, tickling her just enough to make her giggle and beg that he stop. Perfect cover as they came face-to-face with the younger couple in their lounge chairs. Almost in the clear, other than two sets of curious eyes. "Hey, how are ya? Newlyweds, right?"

The guy nodded. "One week." Oh yeah, this dude was definitely trying to decide if he'd really seen what he thought he'd seen. "You guys on your honeymoon too?"

"Yeah. Been on it for every day for the last eight years."

"Aww, that is *so* romantic," the chick said, leaning over to snuggle her newly minted husband. "Isn't it romantic, Clark?" But her hubby didn't get the chance to answer before she forged ahead, her eyes on Derrick, and by default, Hanna. "You have to tell us your secret. I want us to look as happy as the two of you eight years from now."

"Never hold back." Hanna's sweet voice drifted over his shoulder as she beat him to an answer. "Not when you're having a serious conversation and not when you're fucking."

Nothing short of a ball-gag could've kept the laugh from bursting from Derrick's mouth. "Couldn't have said it better myself. And on that note, we'll leave you to enjoy the pool — we certainly did." He put the slack-jawed newlyweds behind them, along with the hottest afternoon he'd ever spent at a pool, regardless of temperature.

"So much for a discreet exit," she said, giving his neck a playful bite.

"Hey, I was all over the discretion thing. You were the one slinging the fuck-talk around."

"I suppose I was. That's *your* influence, Mr. Sutter. You make me misbehave."

"I like it when you misbehave, Mrs. Sutter." Eight years later and he still loved the way that sounded. Marriage—something he'd been thoroughly opposed to, thanks to his absentee mother and abusive drunk of a father—until Hanna.

He snagged a red flower from one of the gardens alongside the path and crouched so she could slide from his back. He knelt on the warm, stone path and tucked the flower under the bikini string riding the sexy curve of her hip. Soft hands rested on his shoulders. Rumpled auburn hair framed the face smiling down at him. The face of an angel. That's how the world saw her, and it fit. Hanna was loving, kind and smart. Too good for him. Always had been, though luckily for him, she refused to see it.

"You look...serious," she said, her smile wavering.

His fault, but easy to fix. "That couple got me thinking about our wedding. How I couldn't stop grinning, even stuck in the damn monkey suit."

"Oh." The smile returned, brighter than ever. "You were totally hot in that tux and you know it."

"Whatever. Nobody was looking at me, baby. All eyes were on you." He curled his hands around her calves. Moved higher, touching every inch of silky skin on the way up. "Watching you walk toward me...I kept wondering how I'd gotten so lucky. And how long I'd have to wait before I could get under that dress."

"So, so bad."

"Oh yeah." He laughed at her halfhearted shove, stood and scooped her hand into his. He brushed the pad of his thumb over the stone in her engagement ring. The only thing he'd been able to afford back then, the small diamond wasn't much to look at. "About time I replaced this with something bigger."

"I love this ring. Besides, size doesn't matter."

"Good thing I'm relatively secure about my manhood."

"Relatively. Uh-huh."

"See, now I'm starting to worry. I'm gonna need reassuring when we get back to the room."

"Translation—blowjob."

"This is why I married a smart girl—for her excellent language skills." An eye roll—she'd pay for that one. He had her over his shoulder in two seconds. She shrieked and giggled from his combination of tickling and spanking for the remainder of the walk to their cabin. He deposited her on solid ground and pulled the keycard from his swim trunks' pocket.

"Oh no, my bag. I left it at the pool and my room key's in it."

"I'll run back and grab it." He kissed the crease between her eyebrows, then pushed the door open. "Go in and get dressed. I promised you shopping, and it's already past three."

"But—what about the blowjob?"

"You'd rather suck my cock than go shopping?" At her nod, his dick went from getting-there to could-poke-an-eye-out rigid. He caught her hand and curled it around his hard-on, grinning when her bottom lip dropped. "You want that in your mouth, my sexy little cock-zombie?"

"You know I do." Down to her knees she went, right there in the open doorway.

The swim trunks rustled and his cock sprang free. "Jesus," he said as her lips closed over the head. The warmth of her mouth surrounded him as she sucked him deeper. All soft and tight and wet. Then the vibrations, god-fucking-damn.

The hum started on his dick. Spread to his balls and some deeper place that made him mindless of everything except for the single fact that his dick was getting sucked. So fucking good. How many times had she blown him—hundreds, thousands? It'd never be enough.

The air-conditioning unit kicked on inside their cabin. Hanna shivered at the rush of cool air. He couldn't resist. A little tug on the ties behind her neck and the bikini top fell away. "Much better."

She shook her head and smiled around his cock. Batted those long, dark eyelashes at him and took every last inch of him down her throat.

He braced himself on either side of the doorframe. Felt as if he could've crushed it in his palms. Had to keep his hands there—if he let go, they'd be on her head, holding her in place while he fucked her mouth. Later.

Except, later it'd be Jer's dick between her lips.

While he watched. While he fucked her pussy, her ass. "Gotta stop..." Shit, she wasn't stopping. "Hanna..." As close as he got to begging. He staggered backward before she sent him hurtling past the finish line.

Some higher power must've intervened, because he had no clue where that dose of willpower had come from. The couple of feet separating them weren't enough. Not with Hanna still on her knees, licking her ruby lips, playing with her nipples. Living proof that heaven and hell *could* exist simultaneously. And that his balls could throb that much harder. "Be dressed by the time I get back with your bag."

"Or what…you'll fuck me so hard, they'll hear me screaming all the way to town?"

"Trying to tempt me with dirty talk?"

"You did say you appreciated my language skills." She shimmied closer. "Want to hear me speak Latin?" She closed her fingers around his cock and blew softly over the engorged, still-moist head. "Fellatio…"

Yeah, shopping could wait.

Chapter Four

Jeremy stared up at the ceiling fan. What a difference a couple hours made. He'd had his doubts about this weekend. How it would impact Derrick and Hanna's marriage, his friendship with D after the fact.

He'd brushed it off as needless speculation because honest to god, he hadn't believed they'd go through with it. Especially after finding them in the middle of an intense moment in the parking lot. But then they'd gone to the pool, during the walk to which Derrick had casually reminded him of the guidelines.

No fucking. No kissing on the mouth. Green light to everything else. And don't forget the main objective—give Hanna a birthday she'd never forget.

He hadn't quite figured out what to do with that level of permission until Hanna walked through the pool gate. That bikini—holy Christ. Her curves. The tumble of dark hair around her shoulders and the nervous-yet-excited smile on her pretty face. Instinct had taken over. He'd touched her and nobody had lost their shit, it'd been fine. He'd sucked her nipples and feasted on her—in front of her husband—and it'd been goddamn phenomenal. He had no doubt that she'd have blown him right there at the pool if that couple hadn't shown up.

He also had no doubt that Derrick had fucked her as soon as he had her out of sight. Hell, Jeremy would've. Knowing Derrick, he probably hadn't waited to get back to their room, either.

Plenty of places en route to their cabin where they could've stopped to screw. Jeremy had spotted a few during his bowlegged walk from the pool. One in particular—a private patch of grass surrounded on three sides by tall flowers. He'd pictured Hanna on her knees there, greedily sucking his cock. Then bent over the small bench, clutching fistfuls of grass while he fucked her from behind. Against the rules, that one, but hey, a man could imagine whatever the hell he wanted, as long as he didn't act on it. And he wouldn't. He'd enjoy all the other benefits of this wild birthday gift to Hanna, then put it behind them. Back to business and friendships as usual on Monday morning.

"Hey." Derrick's gruff voice accompanied a double knock on the door. "I'm taking Hanna into town for some birthday presents, one of which is gonna be a ribbon for your big hard dick."

Couldn't get much louder than that, could he? Not that anybody would've heard. This little resort boasted exclusivity, and it lived up to that promise. Six deluxe cabins scattered on a couple of beautifully landscaped acres meant nobody within earshot for whatever noise the occupants might make. If Hanna was a screamer, no problem. And with that thought, his cock was wide awake. Again. Shit. He pushed off the bed, tucked the damn thing aside the best he could before opening the door.

"Took you long enough." Derrick leaned on the door jamb, grinning like a madman. "Still jerking off?"

"Yeah. Going for the world record."

"Save it for later."

He grunted. Too late for that. "Did you?"

"Hell no. Fucked her in the pool as soon as you left."

"In front of that couple?" he asked, and Derrick grinned even wider. Jeremy bet that decision had more to do with Derrick's need to stay in control than Hanna's need to get laid. Not that he blamed the guy. "Lucky bastard. Never in a million years would Viv have let me do that."

"Did you ever try?" Derrick's question came out casually, but it packed serious punch, whether he'd intended it to or not.

Because no, he hadn't. And sure, he could toss out a lengthy list of reasons for that no, but the bottom line was, he hadn't tried. His attempts to thaw Viv's perpetually frosted vagina had always occurred behind a locked bedroom door with the curtains closed. Maybe he'd have had more success if he'd made the effort under more exciting circumstances. Pointless to wonder—he'd never know now.

"Anyway," Derrick buddy-slapped him back to the present, "we're gonna take off, but we'll be back for that six-thirty dinner reservation. Should be the hottest dinner ever."

"No doubt." Given their plans for Hanna, and after how she'd responded to him—to *them*—earlier, they might trigger the emergency sprinkler system in the resort's small dining room. "Have a good time in town. Spoil her rotten, man."

"That's my plan," Derrick said as he walked away.

Yeah, it'd be his plan too.

The neighboring town was a ten-minute drive from the resort. Close enough to be convenient, far enough to maintain a high level of privacy, as the website had promised. That privacy had certainly come in handy earlier. To think, she'd gone to her knees and sucked Derrick's cock in the doorway of their cabin. Oh, and the pool escapade. Talk about an exciting beginning to the weekend.

For now, though, it was just the two of them. Hanna slid her hand higher up her husband's thigh, smiling when his larger, sturdier hand dropped on top, his fingers lacing with hers. "I love you," she said.

"Love you more, baby."

Normally, she'd argue that point. But Derrick had definitely taken the lead today.

He pulled her little Beetle into an available parking spot on what appeared to be the main drag. The picturesque street stretched farther than she could see, disappearing over a hill several blocks away. Until that point, it was solid with shops and bustling crowds. Beyond the drop-off was a lake view she could've stared at for hours. Calm, blue water met a sky full of puffy, white clouds, the former dotted by sailboats and other small watercraft.

"Ready to shop, birthday girl?"

She blinked up at her husband, waiting on the sidewalk, his hand outstretched in invitation. "We don't have to shop. We could go down to the water and take a walk instead."

"Anything you want. Everything you want." He pulled her up, into his arms, managing to hug her and gently smooth her windblown hair into it proper place in one easy motion. "Tell me where you'd like to start."

"At the beach."

"You got it." He smiled when she slid her arm around his waist. He wrapped an arm around her shoulders, demanding she lean into him as they moved. "You were quiet on the drive over."

"Just thinking."

"Yeah, I saw the smoke."

"Oh stop, it wasn't that bad." She curled her fingertips into his waist, for all the good it did. The man was a rock, nothing fazed him unless he chose to let it. A childhood spent conditioning himself not to show any response to physical and emotional abuse had created that quality.

He pressed a kiss to her temple. "Tell me."

"Okay, but wait until we get past that group of little old ladies."

"So it's gonna be dirty—excellent."

She laughed, but it tapered into a sigh when the time to spill her guts arrived. "You didn't touch me—I mean really touch me—after you got back from the pool or on the drive over here." She burrowed closer, pressing her face tight against the softness of his favorite t-shirt and the warm, hard chest beneath. "Is it because of...earlier?"

"No, baby." He caught her chin and tipped it up, forcing her to look into his eyes. "I promised you this weekend wouldn't change anything about *us*. Trust me to keep that promise."

A ball of tangled emotions lodged in her throat. If she spoke, it'd crack open, and there'd be tears inside. So she nodded. And trusted the man who'd never been anything but one hundred percent honest with her.

They walked the next couple blocks in comfortable silence. Arms wrapped around each other, the late afternoon sun warming their skin, following each other's unspoken cues to window-shop here and there. If they never had hot sex, or any sex, again, it wouldn't matter. Just being together was enough.

He squeezed her tighter then, as if he'd read her mind. "Mind if I duck into a store for something before we head down to the lake? Won't take long."

"Sure, of course. Lead the way."

"Actually, I need to go alone." He winked. "Birthday business." He steered her toward a patch of green space next to the building. "Be right back."

"Derrick…" Arguing would be futile. "Go," she said, shaking her head as she settled on a wrought-iron bench. "But don't go overboard. I don't need things, I just need you."

True to his word, ten minutes later, he was walking toward her. Blue eyes twinkling, a satisfied grin making his dimples pop. God, she couldn't take her eyes off him—a problem shared by the women he passed en route to her location. She didn't blame them one bit.

Hair a little messy because all he'd done to it after the pool was swipe it back with his palm, goatee a bit too long to be trendy, tattoos disappearing beneath the sleeves of his well-worn, white t-shirt. Derrick nailed the bad boy look naturally.

To quote her judgmental mother, he was "rough around the edges". Not inside, where it counted, though her family had never taken the time to find out. As hot as his rough exterior was, his heart and soul were bigger—and belonged to her.

"What's in the bag, mister?" she asked when he dropped onto the bench beside her, his arms casually slung along the back rail.

"Something for my beautiful wife." He nodded at the bag on his lap. "Dig in."

Yes, she'd repeatedly told him not to spend money on her, but since he had… She darted a hand into the small, paper shopping bag and pulled out a tissue-wrapped item that fit nicely in her palm. "What is it?"

"Not telling. Open it."

She could rip into the paper. As with other things, though, much of the fun was in the anticipation. "Give me a clue."

"It's not a vacuum." One of their inside jokes. They knew way too many couples who'd fallen into the cycle of buying each other what Derrick referred to as *passion killers*. Another thing he'd promised would never happen in their relationship.

Given his speed, he'd known exactly what he'd planned to buy, so it had to be something they'd seen in one of the windows. She turned the gift over in her hand. Too small to be any of the useless but pretty decorative things she'd spotted. The wrong shape to be the earrings that had caught her eye. The salesperson had wrapped it very well—Hanna couldn't begin to guess.

"I give up," she said, carefully peeling an edge back.

"Oh good, you're saving the paper." Another wink from her sexy hubby, this one as he mimicked her mother at every gift-swapping occasion, ever.

But she didn't mind. He'd never been anything less than charming and wonderful with her family, despite their unwillingness to extend the same courtesy.

Something metal in shades of copper and silver peeked out from the layers of tissue. Now she really had no idea what he'd bought. She grabbed the edge and ripped. "To hell with the paper."

A husky laugh ripped from his mouth, as expected. It always gave him a kick when she swore outside of sex.

"Oh...it's so pretty." She fingered the edges of the two lovebirds adorning the large hair barrette. Totally her style. And totally unexpected.

"You like it?"

"I love it, it's beautiful. I can't believe I didn't notice it back there."

"Lots of nice stuff in the window — you were probably looking at something else."

She popped it open and slid the bar along her nape. Most barrettes wouldn't hold her thick hair, they either refused to stay fastened or she blew out the pin mechanism trying to force them. She held her breath while clicking the clasp. "It works."

Derrick trailed his fingers down her newly accessible neck. "The woman in the store said the clip part is made of heavier-duty metals than most of the junky crap out there. She swore it'd hold, even after I told her how many of these things you've demolished."

She could picture that conversation, how gruff he would've sounded, complaining in his deep, husky voice about cheap hair accessories. He'd probably left whoever had had the pleasure of serving him a little weak in the knees. Ten years together, and he still had that effect on her. Daily.

She turned slightly, giving him an over-the-shoulder smile as she traced the barrette's design with her fingertips. "How does it look?"

"You make it look beautiful." He cupped her neck — a much gentler touch than when they'd had sex in the pool — and pulled her into his space, half onto his lap. The kiss matched the rest of the moment. Soft, slowed down. But still so, so hot.

The pedestrians and passing cars disappeared from existence. She leaned in, her hands flattened against his chest, her left leg wrapped over his lap. With each sweep of his tongue inside her mouth, every delicious crush of his lips against hers, she needed him more. The ownership that came with his kiss, his hands on her body, the sweet release he always gave her. She slid her thigh higher. So what if passersby could see up her dress?

Derrick's warm palm landed on her bared leg, just above the knee. But it didn't climb. Instead he broke their kiss. "Let's go down to the lake." He chuckled at her frustrated sigh, then circled one of her wrists and brought her hand to the hard-on pushing against his zipper. "Unless you want to take care of that right here?"

* * *

"Tempting..." Hanna said while squeezing his cock. The woman knew she was playing with fire, it was in those gorgeous, whiskey eyes. But she also knew he'd take care of her. Push her limits, but never let her go so far she'd regret anything. Part of why they were perfect together.

So he sat back and let her stroke him through his cargo shorts. Watched her lips part and her tongue peek out as she pressed her clit against his hip. Barely moving, but obviously getting the friction she needed.

Jesus, so fucking hot. A couple more minutes and she'd probably come. She could get off pretty damn discreetly, he'd seen it plenty of times and it made him hornier than hell. He slid his hand up her thigh, under the edge of her dress. High enough to discover she'd gone commando. Of course she had. Now he really had to get them out of here.

He leaned forward so he could whisper in her ear. "Baby, if you come, I'm gonna unzip and push your pretty face down on my cock. Hold it there while you return the favor." Christ, her sexy little moan. Yeah, that kind of *threat* only made her hotter. He needed to change direction. Immediately. "And there's a cop parked across the street."

A quick peek over her shoulder had her scrambling to straighten her dress. "Oh my god, how long has he been there?"

"The whole time." Truth was, the cruiser was empty. The cop had gone down the street and disappeared into a store while she was opening her gift. But Derrick kept that part to himself. Hanna loved riding the edge and relied on him to take her there. He stood, did a bit of straightening of his own, and pulled her to her feet. "Let's go to the beach."

"We should've brought a couple blankets. One to lie on...another to keep us from getting arrested."

"You've got a one-track mind, woman."

"Yes, and you're it." Delicate fingers squeezed his as they walked. "You always will be."

In a couple hours she'd have another man's dick in her mouth and she'd be loving every minute of it, yet he didn't doubt her feelings for him. He pulled her in tighter. Smiled as he patted the little box tucked deep in his pocket. "Ditto, baby. Always."

The street ended at a drop-off. Another street ran parallel to the shoreline below, a boardwalk with short fence lining the escarpment, while the opposite side consisted of wall-to-wall businesses. From the looks of things, this section of town had nothing but food booths and souvenir shops. Good thing he'd asked the manager at the resort where to find a special gift for his wife.

"Are we going down?" she asked, blinking at him innocently.

"Oh yeah." Had to smile at that one, especially when she rolled her eyes. He motioned toward the wide, wooden stairs that led to the beach. "Ladies first."

The embankment wasn't crazy high, but it was steep. As were the steps. If the heel of her sandals snagged in knothole and she fell... He shook off the image. Cut around her to take the lead position. She wasn't prone to clumsiness, but he wasn't taking chances.

She kept her hold on the railing—he could see that much in his peripheral vision, but her other hand landed on his shoulder, near the base of his neck. "My hero."

"You know it."

At the bottom, he followed her lead and removed his shoes. Warm sand filled the gaps between his toes, covered the tops of his feet. Not his favorite sensation. If he'd spent more time at a beach as a kid, maybe he'd get the appeal rather than want to shake his feet off every other second.

Family outings hadn't exactly been his dad's thing—unless you counted a taxi ride to the liquor store on welfare check day. The closest Derrick had come to a beach back then was the overturned skid full of sand in the corner of their backyard. And since every damn cat in the neighborhood used the makeshift sandbox to crap in, it was the last place he would have gone barefoot.

But hate the beach? Never. Not when he got to watch Hanna skipping her way toward the water. Pure joy lit her face when she reached the band of dark, wet sand. That was all the motivation he needed to stop thinking about the shitty past and bolt after her. Loop his arms around her waist and swing her round and round, until her giddy shrieks drew the attention of everyone on the beach.

"Close your eyes," he said as he returned her to the ground. To hell with finding a private area farther along the shoreline. He pulled the box from his pocket and popped the lid open. "Open them."

She zeroed in on the ring immediately. The soft gasp that followed would've been enough, but the smile that went with it made him feel about ten feet tall.

"It's beautiful," her eyes lifted to meet his, "I didn't say anything back there — how did you know?"

"Could've been the fact that your eyes were glued to it the entire time we stood in front of that window."

"Were not," she said with a giggle.

Best sound ever. "Then it must be the other reason."

"Oh?" She snuggled closer, her hands running over his arms, chest and hair, her eyes never straying from his face. As if they were the only people on the beach. On earth. "And what's the other reason?"

He removed the ring from its small velvet case, lifted her right hand and slid the band down her finger. "I know *you*. What you like, what you want. And I'm gonna spend the rest of my life giving you those things."

"Like this weekend."

"Yeah."

She nodded, pulled her lips between her teeth. Cast her eyes down.

He knew those signals. Probably better than she knew them. "Hanna..." He tipped her chin up. Shit, her eyes were all glassy. "I'm fucking this up—you're not supposed to be crying right now."

"Sorry."

"Not supposed to be apologizing either. Fuck." If he were better with words, like her, like everyone else in her life, they'd be doing the tongue tango right now, not having a goddamn impromptu therapy session. "If I could give you what you really want, I would."

"Derrick—"

He shook his head to stop her. "And if the day comes that what we have isn't enough for you, I'll let you go."

"Derrick, please don't—"

This time, he silenced her with a kiss. A reminder that letting her go was the last thing he'd ever want to do. "As long as you want me, I'm here. With you. Nothing and nobody will ever change how much I love you or what we have, I promise. Remember that every time you look at this ring on your finger."

She cupped his face, her fingers playing over his beard in that way of hers that'd convinced him long ago never to shave it off. "I don't need a ring to remind me of that."

"So I should take it back?"

She curled her fingers under protectively. Crushed her hand between their bodies. "Not a chance, mister. It's staying on. Forever."

"Forever works for me, Mrs. Sutter."

Jeremy followed the waiter to a booth at the rear of the resort's intimate dining room. "Just some ice water," he said. "My friends will be here in a few minutes."

Friends. Kind of an understatement this weekend. But that's what they were, both of them. Derrick since they were eight years old, Hanna for the last decade. Hard to believe ten years had passed since that night he and Derrick danced with her at the bar. He'd been physically attracted to her ever since, though it'd waned while Viv was part of his life.

Then Viv had called it quits. Derrick and Hanna had both been there for him. Derrick had listened to him vent, slapped him on the back and said, "Fuck her, she doesn't know what she's giving up." Hanna had offered a female perspective and a soft hand to hold. She'd shared Derrick's sentiment about Viv, minus the cursing. Jeremy appreciated his best friend's support, no question, but the words had sounded a lot better coming from Hanna's lips. And as the pain of the divorce lifted, that longstanding attraction had roared back to the surface.

He froze with his glass halfway to his mouth. This afternoon at the pool, then thinking about Hanna for the past couple hours while he'd pretended to be working on the proposal for his upcoming project, had messed with his neatly organized feelings. It had also redirected most of his blood to his cock. The sight of her standing in the entryway to the resort's intimate dining room finished that job.

A fire-engine-red dress hugged her exquisitely feminine body. Mile-high heels made her legs look sexier than ever. Her shiny, reddish-brown hair was pulled back, showing off her kissable neck. One of the many parts he was allowed to kiss this weekend. He sure as hell planned to take advantage of the opportunity, even though he'd tried to talk Derrick out of the idea initially. Yeah, not as wholeheartedly as he could or should have, but he had tried. Now that he'd had a taste of Hanna, now that he knew exactly what was under that dress and how naturally she'd responded to him...damn. Going back to being her *friend* on Monday was going to be hell.

Derrick grinned at him while sliding an arm around his wife's waist. Possessive and protective of her, always. Never enough to make him an asshole, but not leaving the world with any doubt Hanna was *his* woman, either. Jeremy didn't blame the guy one bit.

Christ. Time he focused strictly on the physical. A couple hours from now, this gorgeous woman would be sucking him off — probably more than once before the night ended. He'd work on rewiring his brain after checking out tomorrow. Tonight he was going to enjoy Hanna to the fullest extent of the rules.

"Hey, you two." He stood when they reached the table, pulling his chair aside so Hanna could slide onto the curved bench of their private, corner booth. She watched, wide-eyed, as he took the spot beside her, rather than resume his former single seat. Her eyes went wider still when he stretched his arm over the back of the bench with his hand not-so-subtly brushing her shoulder. "Have a good time shopping?"

Hanna's mouth opened, but all that came out was, "Um..."

Derrick chuckled and dropped into the chair immediately to her left — the seat Jeremy had vacated. "We had a great afternoon. Took a walk along the main drag, bought my beautiful wife a couple presents, fucked her on the beach in front of a few dozen people."

"You did not." She leaned forward to give Derrick a playful push on the shoulder, then fell back into position close to Jeremy. Very close. "He didn't. You believe me, not him, right?"

"Of course."

Derrick snorted. "Suck up."

"Smart," he said, and Derrick snorted a second time. Jeremy trailed his fingers along Hanna's shoulder. Something electric sparked between them— he felt it all the way to his knees, saw it in the depths of her golden-brown eyes. "But I'm not above sucking up. Whatever the lady wants, she gets."

"Can every weekend be my birthday?" The bubbly tone of voice suggested her question was innocently rhetorical.

The idea of this arrangement becoming a recurring thing, though... That'd be a dangerous proposition. One he wouldn't turn down if the opportunity presented itself.

He twirled a loose strand of her long hair around his finger. He didn't tug, yet she gravitated closer. Destroying him, she was, and they hadn't even ordered dinner yet. He smiled at her while keeping Derrick in his peripheral vision. Any sign that he'd crossed a line and he'd back off. If he saw the sign. Her soft skin and the subtle scent of her shampoo were already proving to be one hell of a distraction. Not to mention the lack of blood flowing to his brain.

"Show Jer what you got."

"Okay." She practically bounced on the spot. She leaned forward and turned, her fine-boned fingers smoothing over that gorgeous hair he planned to wrap around his fist later. "First he surprised me with this beautiful barrette."

"Very pretty."

"Isn't it?" she asked, resuming her position under his arm. She lifted her right hand, wiggling the fingers in front of his face. "And when we got down to the beach, he gave me this ring." A soft sigh slipped from her lips. "I told him not to spend more money on me—this weekend is expensive enough—but it's so…perfect."

"Derrick has good taste."

His buddy nodded. In thanks, sure, but more likely in acknowledgement. He'd know Jeremy's comment had nothing to do with his choice of gifts and everything to do with the woman he'd chosen. That they'd both chosen. Damn coin toss.

Derrick tracked Jeremy's fingers as they moved over Hanna's skin. His cool, blue eyes lifted, met Jeremy's and locked. Reading his mind, probably, or as close to it as truly possible. Twenty-plus years of brother-like friendship had honed that skill. Instead of reaching across the table and slugging him, Derrick nodded again, then his full attention returned to the beautiful woman between them. Surreal. All of it.

Jeremy laughed—a bit too loudly for the small room with its ten-or-so tables and handful of guests. Hanna smiled, albeit in a startled kind of way, and Derrick's blond eyebrows rose. Might as well share his thoughts, they'd be sharing a lot more than words later.

"I was thinking about our pact from way back—that we'd never let a woman come between us. We broke that deal today, D, literally."

"Yeah, I guess we did." Derrick leaned forward, one arm on the table and one beneath. A couple seconds later, Hanna's breath hitched. "And we're gonna break it again. Many, many times."

"Can I interest you in dessert, coffee, tea...?" A standard part of any waiter's job, but this guy had been extra attentive throughout their meal. Not surprising, given the exclusivity of the resort—and the picture the three of them undoubtedly made.

Side-by-side in close proximity, she and Jeremy must have looked like a couple. However, Derrick had moved his chair tight to the left side of the bench, and his arm lay on the table, his hand curled atop hers. Plus, a person would have to be blind to miss the way he looked at her. And they wore wedding bands, whereas Jeremy did not. Hanna bet the waiter had been trying to figure out the dynamic all evening.

"The choice is yours, birthday girl. Interested in some dessert?" Such innocent words from Jeremy. His hand beneath the table, presently occupied with making lazy circles over her clit—not so innocent.

She needed out of this restaurant. Immediately. "Just the check." Emboldened by Derrick's gruff chuckle, she added, "We'll have dessert back in the room."

"I'll take the bill here," Jeremy said, dismissing the waiter with a curt nod.

"Yes, sir," he mumbled before turning away. He had to know something was going on under the table. That many somethings had been going on under there throughout the meal.

Derrick and Jeremy had spent the last hour making her crazy. Oh sure, there'd been normal conversation. But there's also been dirty talking. Physical teasing that took her to the brink of orgasm over and over — sometimes just one of them, sometimes both of them. Like now. Derrick leaned forward. His fingers walked up her inner thigh. Slowly, his eyes intent on her face as he inched closer to his target.

She shook her head, tried to squeeze her thighs closed. As if that would dissuade her husband. A wickedly determined grin brought out the dimples in his cheeks. He didn't need to use physical force to regain access. One sexy smile and her legs parted willingly.

"That's my girl." Two long fingers slid inside, then curled toward a spot he knew oh-so well.

Only the return of the wide-eyed waiter saved her from another torturous brush with satisfaction. She pushed both probing hands from her lap, inadvertently moving the tablecloth away in the process. A quick downward glance revealed her hiked-up dress and more than a sliver of skin. And hers wasn't the only gaze glued to her bared private parts. Oh god.

Derrick yanked the linen until it covered her, rattling the dishes on the table. His barked, "Hey — eyes up here," got the waiter's attention plenty fast.

"Sorry." The guy winced at Derrick's *I could rip your arms off with my teeth* expression. He scrambled to grab the credit card Jeremy held in his upturned fingers, nearly dropping it in a glass. "I'll uh…"

"Be right back?" Jeremy's voice was cool and smooth, as always.

"Yes, sir," the waiter glanced at the platinum card in his hand, "Mr. Cruz."

More than ever, she wanted to be back in their room. With Derrick. The man who had roared to her defense, as he always did. Even now, with the waiter across the room, Derrick's jaw clenched and ticked. Her parents often described his love as ferocious. They always meant it negatively — they couldn't be more wrong.

"If you two don't mind, I'm going to wander back to the cabin and freshen up."

As she'd known he would, Derrick pushed his chair away, stood and took her hand to help her from the booth. "I'll walk you." He draped an arm over her shoulders, kissing the top of her head when she melted against his side. "Don't tip too much. Eyeballing Hanna was tip enough."

"Agreed." Jeremy smiled in his easy, confident way. "Catch up with you shortly."

* * *

Derrick glared at the waiter as they exited the restaurant. Little weasel had the good sense not to look at them as they passed. Wasn't really the bastard's greedy eyes that had him riled, though. He'd lost control of the situation back there, and because of that slip, Hanna had been embarrassed. He liked pushing her limits, watching color flood her cheeks when she rode a thrill. Not from humiliation. Worse, he could've prevented it.

"You okay?" he asked.

"Better now that we're out of there."

Shit.

She stopped in the middle of the path, wrapped her arms around his neck and squeezed. "You were too far away for me to do that. Or this..." Soft, warm lips met his. Her tongue teased its way between his lips, drew his into her mouth.

Well, damn. All right. He cupped her ass and pulled her tighter. Pressed the hard-on he'd endured throughout dinner against her abdomen. Heat flared at the back of his neck where her nails dug in. Fuck yeah. A throaty moan that meant she was seriously turned-on filled his mouth, his head. Nearly made him lose his fucking mind.

"Cabin. Now," he muttered against her lips. "Can't do the things I need to do to you here."

A little shimmy and her shoes clattered against the cobblestone. She knelt to collect them, then grabbed his hand. "Let's go."

Hanna's dress made running impossible. They did their best—a semi-trot that would've made an old man's jogging look like an Olympian sprint. Hanna's giggle carried on the fresh air of a beautiful summer evening. Didn't matter how slow they moved, they might as well have been flying. That's what she did to him. Made him light. Made the simple stuff amazing.

Yeah, getting her naked could wait a few more minutes. "This way," he said, dragging her off the path. "Shortcut." Total bullshit. They cut behind another of the cabins, wove around a small garden. Down a narrower path that didn't have a signpost. He'd planned to show her his find tomorrow morning, but waiting had never really been his thing. *Now* always seemed like the best time. Especially with her.

"Um, I don't think this is a shortcut to our room…"

"Worried we're gonna get lost?"

"Not even a little."

Zero bullshit in that answer. She'd hopped on the back of his bike more times than he could count, often not knowing where they were headed, always trusting him to find their way. He slowed to a normal walking pace, lifted her hand to his lips. Brushed his beard over her soft skin. That always made her smile, even when things weren't in down-and-dirty mode. This little detour should have the same effect.

A couple more minutes of walking took them to the end of the path—and their destination. He let go of her hand, then hung back to watch.

"Oh, Derrick...this is so pretty." She swept the trailing boughs of the huge, weeping willow tree aside and stepped beneath its canopy.

Lucky thing the sun hadn't gone down yet. The tree itself was something to see—had to be one of the biggest of its kind he'd seen up close—but it was the combination of light and leaves that made it amazing. Something he'd known she'd love the second he saw it.

"It reminded me of that picture on the mantel at your grandparents' house."

She spun around, her eyes wide and locked with his. "The one with me sitting in the crook of their old wishing tree when I was twelve?"

"Yeah."

"They haven't had that picture on display since they moved to the seniors' complex, and that was three years ago."

"Don't need to see it," he tapped his temple, "have it stored up here." Along with her dreamy expression anytime she'd talked about her childhood visits to her grandparents' former estate. How much she'd loved sitting under that tree, listening to frogs and birds, watching the sun bounce off the small stream that ran alongside. Like something from a storybook.

She crooked a finger at him. "Get over here."

A command he was happy to obey. He followed her under, though "inside" might've been a better description. Stepping beneath the tree felt like entering a private little world. The sun's rays pushed through the swaying branches. The grass beneath her bare feet could've been an intricately designed carpet, covered with abstract patterns in multiple shades of green. Ovals of light danced over her skin, hair and dress. The place had already had a magical quality. Hanna standing in the middle of it, her face glowing as she took it in, pretty much rendered him speechless. A damn mighty feat.

"You're amazing. When did you find this place?"

"Went for a walk while you were getting ready for dinner. It was that or join you in the shower."

"I wouldn't have objected to having you wash my back, you know."

He grunted. "Yeah, because *that's* what would've happened."

A couple of steps and she stood in front of him, palms flat on his chest. "I wouldn't have objected to anything."

"I know." Fuck, did he ever. So did his damn cock, which currently felt thicker than the willow tree's massive trunk. "That's why I went for the walk."

She giggled and wrapped her arms around his waist, pressed her cheek to his chest. "Since you found this beautiful spot, I guess I won't complain."

For a few minutes he just held her. Closed his eyes and listened to the cicadas and tree frogs doing their thing. Tried to imagine what it must've been like to grow up the way she did, with freedom and places to daydream. People who'd be waiting with open arms and an encouraging smile when she went home. She and Jeremy had that in common.

Not that Jer's mom hadn't tried to give Derrick a taste of that life. Linda Cruz had done more for him than anybody—starting with the call to social services when he'd shown up in her third-grade classroom with bruises his ratty clothes didn't cover. His previous teachers had obviously chosen to turn a blind eye, because they sure as shit couldn't have missed the endless marks he'd sported on a regular basis.

When going through proper channels failed, Mrs. Cruz had taken the less official road. She'd brought him to her house under the guise of free tutoring, introduced him to her son of the same age—Jeremy—then turned him loose in her home and yard. To play. To be a kid. Several times a week for the better part of the school year, 'til his dad demanded his child laborer and resident punching bag be home more often. But man, it'd been good while it lasted.

"You're so quiet."

"Ten years together and I can still shock you." He held her tight, chuckling at her attempt to dig those dangerous elbows into his kidneys once again. "I was thinking. Even us dirt-under-the-fingernails types do that sometimes."

"Don't do that..."

Yeah, stupid comment. One she, of all people, didn't deserve. He kissed the top of her head. Rubbed his beard over it, knowing he'd mess her smoothly pulled-back hair and not giving a rat's ass, because neither would she. "When you hung out at your grandparents' place as a kid, under that willow, what did you wish for?"

"Hmm...depends on my age at the time. Could've been wishing unicorns were real or wishing that Bruce McGinnis would ask me to be his girlfriend."

He found her hand and wove their fingers together so they could walk side by side. "I know how the first part worked out. Sorry about the unicorns."

"Hey, they could be real. I just haven't seen one yet."

So fucking sweet. Good thing he hadn't met her when they were younger. He'd been a little shithead more often than not back then – she'd have hated him and he wouldn't have all this.

"I want you to say it."

He led her to the edge of the grass, smiling when she let go so she could tiptoe into the shallow brook that ran alongside. "Say what, baby?"

"That you believe unicorns could be real."

Under other circumstances, he would've laughed his ass off – solely to get her to attack him – then fucked her until she'd forgotten the reason for her attack. But she looked so damn beautiful standing there, ankle-deep in the clear, sparkling water, dressed for sin but with eyes full of innocence. As if she truly believed horses with a single, pointy horn in the middle of their face existed somewhere.

Only one way he could answer. "Unicorns could be real." Damn, that smile. For him. Because she loved *him*. That right there was proof that anything was possible. "What about Bruce – did he ever make his move?"

"Yes."

Well, look at that. Cheeks so red, they almost matched her dress. "There's a story there."

"Nothing exciting."

"Something smells like bullshit..." With a quick flick of his thumb he'd shucked his shoes. He didn't bother to roll the bottoms of his jeans, just waded in after her. "And I think it's your story."

Oh, she tried to deke around him and back onto dry ground. Didn't succeed though. He caught her around the waist and scooped her up, kicking and giggling, full of playful squirming. Until he faked dropping her into the water.

"Don't." She clamped her arms behind his neck when he mock-fumbled a second time. "You wouldn't..."

She had to know that he would. In fact, suggesting that he *wouldn't* douse her only made him want to do it more. A fact that was most certainly written all over his face right now.

"Derrick, please don't...remember it's my birthday weekend."

"The ring, hair clip and a threesome aren't enough? I think your birthday card has run out of gimmes, baby. The only way you walk away from this in a dry dress is by telling me the thing you don't want to tell me about old Brucie."

She shook her head. Shrieked and held on for dear life when he pretended to launch her downstream. "All right, I'll tell, but set me down on the grass first."

"Nice try." Not losing control of this situation, no chance.

"Bully."

"Just the way you like me." Nails dug into his trapezius and the heat between them shot up about fifty degrees. "Isn't that right?"

Now she nodded, licking her lips greedily as she did so. "I had a crush on Bruce since the sixth grade, but he was two years older and didn't know I existed."

"Until...?"

"Until I was in tenth grade. He noticed me at a dance and uh, invited me to cut out and go back to his house. We weren't alone but it wasn't a party, either. Just a couple of his buddies and their steady girlfriends. Me, a handful of seniors and a case of illegally acquired beer. My mother would have died if she'd found out."

No shit on that one. He could totally picture the scenario. Had a pretty good idea how this story ended too. And it had his blood fucking boiling. "Don't tell me he took advantage of you."

"No, nothing like that." She must have sensed the sharp change to his mood, because she stroked his face and looked into his eyes as she spoke. "They were all very nice. Nobody pressured me to do anything, drinking or otherwise."

He nodded. Let her touch and words sooth the protective rage that'd roared to the surface at the thought of what could have happened.

"So..." One pretty, dark eyebrow rose. "I guess I'm off the hook for telling the rest of the story."

Boom—with that challenge, she'd defused him. Pulled him back to the playfulness this moment deserved.

He grinned and shook his head. "Nice try. Let me guess, you hadn't had alcohol before that night."

"God no. I was fifteen."

The innocence, Jesus. Beer was old hat by the time he'd hit tenth grade. He'd moved on to cheap vodka and assorted small-time drugs, paid for by hocking shit he stole from naïve princesses like Hanna. "What happened—you got drunk and gave it up?"

"Not quite."

"This I gotta hear."

"I had one beer, which I hated."

He grinned wider. She still wrinkled her cute nose at the stuff. "And?"

"Everybody hung out in the living room and talked for a while. Then all the other couples disappeared behind various closed doors. I'd had a crush on Bruce for years, so I said yes when he asked if I wanted to go to his room. We got on the bed and started making out. He rolled onto his back so I was on top. We still had our clothes on and we were kissing like crazy. It was…"

The color of her cheeks told him he had to hear the rest of this story. "Yeah?"

"A lot more fun than I'd imagined."

Oh yeah, he remembered those days. Classic teenage stuff. "Good old dry-humping."

The blush that'd started to fade flared to a fresh shade of deep pink. "Yes, until I, um…"

"What? Did you puke on him or something?"

"Worse." She pressed her forehead against his shoulder. "I had an orgasm."

His hoot carried across the quiet summer evening. "Nicely done, Bruce. He must've felt like a fucking king, making you come. Took years for me to unlock the mystery that is the female orgasm, and to be honest, I never tried at that age. Didn't even cross my mind."

"I don't know how he felt, I jumped off the bed and ran out."

"Oh man, poor Bruce." He sputtered when she squirmed in his arms and the hard ball of her heel connected with the soft spot below his ribs. "That's not very ladylike, you know. Why'd you run, anyway?"

"I was totally freaked out. I'd never had an orgasm before."

"You mean never with a guy, right?" he asked while returning her to the grassy haven beneath the willow's branches.

"No, I mean *never* never. I'd touched myself a little, once in a while, and I knew how to make it feel sort-of good, but never taken it all the way. I was terrified I'd scream like one of the porno chicks I'd seen on my friend's computer, and my parents would hear and send me off to a convent or something."

He shouldn't laugh. Couldn't stop it from happening though. The harder he tried not to laugh, the less control he had, and the more contagious the laughter became.

He fucking loved that sound—Hanna dissolving into a fit of giggles. Almost made him want to ditch their plans for tonight and hang out under this tree, see what other gems he could pry from his beautiful wife. They'd have to come back another time. Or plant a willow tree in their yard.

She dropped onto the grass in a particularly sun-spotted area. "I can't believe you made me relive that."

"I can't believe I'm just hearing that story now." He took the spot directly behind her and pulled her between his legs, wrapping his arms around her waist. "Gonna have to see if that guy's on Facebook when we get home. Check out my competition."

"Pfft. You don't have any competition. You haven't had any since our first night together."

"That's how it's gonna stay too. Because unlike Bruce McWhatever-His-Name was, I won't let you grind'n'run. Got about thirty-thousand orgasms to give you before I'm done."

"Is that all?"

"I figure that's about two a day, every single day for the next forty-or-so years. Not enough to keep you satisfied?"

"I suppose I can make do with that." She rested her head against his chest, tipping it up to smile up at him. "This isn't my grandparents' old wishing tree, but it's close. Want to know what I'm wishing for right now?"

"If it's for me to find you a unicorn, I may have to scale back on that thirty-K estimate. Hunting fairytale creatures could get time consuming."

"I'm willing to forego the unicorn so you have more time to focus on thirty thousand better things. Which takes me back to my current wish…" She turned and rose on her knees, those soft hands gently gripping his shoulders. "I wish you'd take me to our room and start chipping away at that number."

He took his time. Let his eyes wander over every inch of the sexy sight before him. "I can do that." Oh yeah, he definitely could.

Chapter Five

After settling the tab from dinner, Jeremy had gone back to his cabin to make some necessary phone calls. One to say goodnight to his son—that was never a hardship—and a couple work-related check-ins that couldn't wait until Monday. He'd cleared the decks as much as possible for this weekend, but with an overseas project involving millions of dollars, he couldn't truly step away, not even for a day. Now he stood outside Derrick and Hanna's cabin. Their dark, empty cabin.

Knowing those two, they'd detoured off the cobblestone path for some immediate gratification. He checked his watch. They'd left the restaurant about forty minutes ago. Either Derrick was doing some tantric thing or they'd fallen asleep behind a shrub somewhere. Ten years together and they still fucked like newlyweds. Hell, probably more than most newlyweds.

With that thought, they came into view. Leisurely strolling along the path. Arms wrapped around each other. A big, easy smile on Derrick's face, Hanna practically glowing. So obviously in love. Happy together.

What the hell was he doing, getting in the middle of that? Jeremy grunted. He wouldn't be in the middle, Hanna would. He was just here to serve as a bookend. A bookend who'd be getting his cock sucked by a gorgeous woman he'd always been attracted to, and who wanted him here. And yeah, his pants just got noticeably tighter.

"Sorry we kept you waiting." Hanna smiled at him, though her arms stayed around her husband. "We went for a walk and lost track of time."

"Not a problem, I just got here. Had some business calls to make so my cell doesn't ring tonight."

Derrick laughed. "Don't worry, buddy..." His fingers lazily stroked Hanna's shoulder. "You'll be too distracted to hear the damn thing buzzing."

Fucking right he would. All night long. "So. A walk, huh?" He let his eyes linger on Hanna's face—her full, richly colored lips, the pert little nose, those big, golden-brown eyes. "Sure you weren't having dessert without me?"

Her cheeks bloomed pink. Goddamn, so beautiful. "We didn't sneak any dessert. Derrick found a tree he knew I'd want to see, because it'd remind me of something special from my childhood." She planted a chaste kiss on her husband's bearded chin. "But I'm sure you're aware his sweet, thoughtful side after all your years together."

After having his fingers inside Hanna at the restaurant, Derrick had taken her to see a tree. Not to fuck her against the tree, but to *look* at it, for some old time's sake. Jeremy glanced from Hanna to Derrick, who just shrugged and smiled—the smile of a man who had everything he wanted and full confidence he wouldn't lose it. Lucky bastard.

"Anyway..." Hanna disentangled herself and took a few sexy steps in Jeremy's direction. Any concerns he'd had a few minutes earlier vanished when she trailed a finger over his Adam's apple and into the unbuttoned section of his shirt. "We're all here now."

"At your birthday party." No worrying about permission from here out. He put his hands on her as if he had every right doing so. Ran his palms over the curves of her waist, hips and ass. Caught her wrist and cupped her hand over his fly. "No birthday cake, that's your dessert. Want it?"

"Yes." She squeezed, harder than Viv ever would've handled him, the touch of a woman who was plenty comfortable with the male anatomy.

"Do you believe her?" Derrick took position behind his wife, his hands resting on her shoulders. "I think she should prove it." A bit of pressure to those bare, feminine shoulders and Hanna was on her way down.

To her knees. Then unzipping his pants, popping the button. Freeing his cock.

All he could do was stare. At her fingers as they coiled around him, her lips, parted and advancing on his cock, her tongue lapping at his slit.

She tilted her head a little, enough to look up at him with her wide, amber eyes. Fuck, a man could get lost in those eyes.

If he could see them. Derrick's hand entered Jeremy's field of vision. It spanned the back of Hanna's head, not pushing exactly, but most certainly sending a message. *Get to work.* And Christ, she did exactly that. Her shiny lips sealed over the head of his cock, then slid down, down, all the way to the base. She hummed, gave him suction. So fucking good.

"Fingers out of your pussy, baby—that's our job." Derrick's voice brought Jeremy back to his senses. Sort of. "I think she's ready for us to take her inside."

A downward glance confirmed Derrick's description. Hanna's free hand was between her legs, and her eyes, looking up at him once again, were dilated and glassy. From a minute, maybe less, of sucking him. Oh hell yes, they needed to take her inside. Immediately.

* * *

The heavy cabin door clicked closed behind them. One of the guys hit the light switch and a small table lamp came to life. The first thing that caught her attention—the bed. Of course. It was really going to happen, right now, in this room. Hanna turned to face them. Derrick with his longish, blond hair and goatee, dressed in a t-shirt, jeans and all his beautiful ink. Beside him—dark-haired, clean-shaven Jeremy, dressed to impress in black pants and a crisp, white shirt, its sleeves rolled to the elbows. What a view. Two gorgeous men—so different from one other, but both unbelievably hot. And both of them obviously hungry—for her.

"I need a minute to get ready."

"Go ahead, we'll wait," Derrick said as he locked the cabin door. "Unless you want us to come in there and help."

Oh, the things they could do to "help" in the neighboring luxury bathroom... She shook her head emphatically, garnering a sexy grin and chuckle from her husband.

"Get going then. I said we'd wait, I didn't say we'd do it patiently."

She grabbed her lingerie bag and headed for the open door. She flicked on the bathroom light but paused before going inside. "Your clothes stay on until I take them off. Got it?"

"Enjoy this moment of control, baby. Once we get you on your knees again, we're taking it back."

No comment from Jeremy, just a lethally sexy smile and twinkling, dark-brown eyes. Maybe dirty talk wasn't his thing. Or maybe he just needed some female motivation. She'd be sure to give him some tonight.

Behind the closed door, she peeled off the dress with shaking hands. Then the bra. The huge mirror above the double vanity reflected her naked body. She shouldn't be nervous—between the pictures and video Derrick had taken to show Jeremy, and how much of her had been exposed at the pool—Jeremy had already seen it all. Somehow that didn't help the butterflies in her stomach. She hadn't gotten truly naked with anybody aside from Derrick since they met. And while her body was decent enough, she wasn't exactly dedicated to exercise, as the men in the other room were. Derrick had no problem with some booty and boob jiggle. Hopefully Jeremy felt the same.

A laugh ripped in the next room. She pressed her ear to the door, which netted her some muffled talking. The only way to know what they were talking and laughing about would be to go in there. And there went those pesky butterflies again.

She ran water for a bath, sliding into the massive tub as soon as she had the temperature perfect. The water rose around her, tickling her inner thighs, then her breasts as it lapped against her skin. She took care of the utilitarian aspects of this dip, including shaving her legs for the second time today. Intentionally delaying her exit, yes. Because what they were about to do beyond that door was so much more than what'd happened at the pool. A dozen things could go wrong. Or everything could go amazingly right. She honestly wasn't sure which possibility she feared most.

"Hey..." Derrick's voice accompanied a quick tap on the door, which he opened without waiting for her reply. His head and one shoulder slipped through the crack he'd created. He homed in on her nipples where they peeked through a thin layer of bubbles and gave her the hubba-hubba eyebrows. "Think that tub would fit three?"

She glanced at the available space. "Um, not without one of us—at least—slipping and breaking something."

"I'd take my chances." More of his hunky frame entered the room. "The slope and height at the end of that tub looks about right for bending you over while you suck Jer's dick. We get you positioned over one of those jets and it'll be better than your vibrator." He cocked his head, clearly working out the logistics in that perfectly dirty mind of his. "Yeah, I'm thinking this could work."

"Oh no, I'm done in here." She scrambled from the tub, nearly wiping out on the tiled floor in the process.

"Whoa..." He caught her before she totally splatted. He righted her, his hands sliding over her suds-slicked arms and back. Down to her ass, of course, which he cupped as he pulled her solidly against him. "Good thing I was here to catch you."

"It's your fault I fell."

"Almost fell, since I saved you. Plus, your claim is bullshit."

"Is not." The argument of a simpleton, but thinking and speaking intelligently had gone down the drain with the bathwater the moment his fingers ventured between her legs.

"Is too." He winked, then nodded toward the puddle she'd made beside the tub. "You didn't put down a towel or the bathmat. And that was long before I walked in."

"Shit." Not that she always needed to be right, but there were times she really hating being proven wrong.

"Such a dirty mouth. I love it."

She issued him a *hmph* and wiggled free of his arms. Waggled her fingers at him to shoo. "Get out of here so I can transform myself from adorable to irresistible."

"Baby, you are *always* that." Rather than turn around, he walked backward to the door, ravishing her with his eyes as he went. "Five minutes," he said before closing the door.

No need to ask what'd happen if she exceeded the allotted time. His lust-laden grin answered that question.

She toweled off, moisturized, refreshed her makeup and brushed her teeth in record time. She pulled the remaining items from the bag. The barely-there panties Megan had gawked at, plus some accessories her bestie hadn't seen.

Such as the beaded anal toy. She squirted a couple drops of lube onto the tip of the short, flexible toy and watched them slide down over the smallest of five adjoining balls. Ass man that he was, Derrick would enjoy finding—and removing—these.

She leaned over the counter and reached between her legs. She bit down on her bottom lip as she pushed the first bead past her rim. The first breach always felt so good. She teased the next, larger bead inside, then the next. God, two more to go and she already felt their presence. Already wanted to rub her clit until she came, which would take about thirty seconds. She rocked against the air as she slid the remainder of the beads inside.

She stood straight—oh god. She grabbed the edge of the sink, focused on her breathing. On anything but the beads filling her or the tingling hum of need brewing low in her core.

She stepped into the panties next. From the front, they looked like any other skimpy thong. Not from the back, though. She twisted so she could see her backside and arranged the rows of thin, black ribbons across her backside. The pink finger-loop of the probe peeked out from between her ass cheeks. Yup, not bad. Pretty damn sexy, if she did say so.

Lastly—the jewelry. What a find these had been. She'd finally worked up the nerve to stop at a body piercing salon and book an appointment to have her nipples done. But the very sweet—and equally yummy—piercer she'd spoken with had sensed her fear. He'd suggested she try non-pierced rings until she could look at the piercing equipment without turning six shades of green. She'd almost worn the pretty rings for Derrick—several times—instead of saving them for tonight. Somehow, she'd managed some self-restraint. Not an easy task around her husband. But it'd be worth it.

She positioned the first silver, filigree ring over her nipple. Then the second one. She gave each nipple a tug to draw the hard peaks higher through the center openings. Voilà, done. *So* pretty and sexy. They felt good, too, just tight enough to create a subtle, spreading heat.

She did a little shimmy in front of the mirror to ensure everything would stay put. Check and check. She slipped on the black suede stilettos she'd borrowed from Megan and took one last look. Heart pounding madly within her chest, she opened the door to what would undoubtedly be the hottest birthday party ever.

* * *

Jesus, she was beautiful. Yeah, he'd thought that every day for the last ten years, and yeah, he was biased because he'd been madly in-fucking-love with her every one of those days, but damn. He glanced over at Jeremy. Dude's mouth was practically on the floor, and that was saying something for a guy with Jeremy's composure.

"Aren't you going to sing me 'Happy Birthday'?"

"Safe to say we'll do anything you want right now, baby."

"I'll second that," Jeremy said. "But I think we can find better ways to celebrate than singing."

Her eyes moved back and forth between them. A deep-pink blush covered her cheeks, it'd even crept down her neck to the upper part of her chest. Hard to believe she was embarrassed or nervous after what they'd already done today. Maybe it wasn't the doing part, just how to get started. He could help with that.

"C'mere." Derrick opened his arms and, boom, she was there. "Hey, beautiful." He cupped her face and kissed her until she sighed into his mouth. Didn't want her getting too relaxed. He eased back a bit. Pushed away the hair that'd settled in front of her shoulders so he could feast his eyes on her tits and their shiny new decorations. He brushed his thumbs over the hard nubs standing in the middle of the silver rings. "These are fucking incredible. Do they hurt?"

"No, they're tight, but it's a good, tingly sensation."

"You have to show me where you got them so I can buy you more stuff like this." He dipped down and flicked a nipple with his tongue. Caught it between his teeth and tugged the way he knew made her instantly hot. "Maybe something with clamps or chains."

Her lips parted, but she didn't get to respond.

The next words came from Jeremy, as he moved in behind her. "Oh, man, D...I've got one hell of a view back here."

"Can't be better than mine."

Jeremy whistled, long and low. "Have a look before you decide."

He rolled his tongue around her other nipple. Gave it a sharp nip that made her gasp—and press her tit against his mouth. "Turn around and let Jer appreciate my view, while I see what other surprises you've got for me."

She did as instructed, slower than he would've thought possible, hips swaying side to side in the process. When that sexy ass of hers was in his sight, he knew why. And yeah, it was one hell of a view.

He dropped to his haunches. Smoothed his palms over her lower back, her hips, the inside of her thighs. Saving the best for last. One at a time, he traced the four, thin bands of black that spanned her ass. He curled his hands over the top strip and eased them down.

"These are fucking hot, but they're gonna be in my way." He lifted each foot and pulled the panties from her body. He trailed both hands up the inside of her legs, rubbed two fingers from one over her clit while he slid the index finger of his other hand through the looped end of an anal toy and gave it a jiggle. "This is new."

"Yes," she said in a breathless voice. Then, "God, yes, harder, do it harder."

That last part wasn't for him. A glance upward revealed the reason for her begging — Jeremy's head moving back and forth between her tits. Not biting her hard enough. Much as Derrick wanted her to enjoy this experience, he kinda liked that Jeremy didn't know all her secrets. No doubt his friend would figure out some tonight. But not all. Hanna would still belong to him.

"Better give her what she wants, Jer." He certainly planned to. He slid his fingers back and pushed two inside her pussy while wiggling the loop of the toy with his other hand. Whatever the toy was, it was big enough that he felt it moving. Ridged — no, bumpy. And long. He added another finger and she moaned above him. Hell, he joined in. "Gonna fuck you so deep, baby. You're not gonna know where I end and you begin."

"Please…" She whimpered when he removed his fingers and stood.

"Soon," he whispered in her ear from behind. He circled her wrist and brought her hand to the front of his jeans. "You gotta unwrap your presents first."

* * *

Jeremy had always loved breasts. Hanna's were amazing, and with the silver rings fastened around the base of her nipples, pushing them high and hard for the taking, Christ, he could enjoy them for hours. But when she found his zipper and slid it down, all he could think about was her mouth. Wrapped around his cock. Immediately.

To hell with her earlier request. He went to work on his buttons, stripped the shirt off while she divested him of pants, boxers and socks. Despite the urgency and heat swirling around them, he had to laugh.

"Something funny?" she asked, sliding her fist up and down his rock-hard shaft.

"The socks."

"There's a scientific reason why I removed them," she said.

Behind her, Derrick chuckled. "Just go with it."

She looked over her shoulder at her husband. "You don't believe the research?"

"Baby, I'm all for research. We can do our own official study at home." Derrick caught her by the chin and kissed her, long and thoroughly.

The pressure on Jeremy's cock increased. So did her speed. Fuck, he was going to explode. "What's the reason?" He focused on speaking, not his hips involuntarily pumping into her fist.

She tore her mouth away and looked him in the eye. "Research shows that wearing socks makes you orgasm faster." She winked, then went to her knees in front of him. "And I don't want that. I want your cock in my mouth as long as possible before you come down my throat."

Fuck. That pretty, dirty-talking mouth hovered over the head of his cock. So close. Not close enough.

"She's waiting, buddy." Derrick peeled off his t-shirt and the rest, until he stood naked behind his kneeling wife. "Tell her what you want."

This was insane. He gripped his cock at the base, holding it straight for her. "Suck it. All of it."

Her hands landed on his hips. Electricity rocketed through his body at the first touch of her lips on his shaft. He wanted to look. To watch his cock disappear into her mouth. But it was too much, too hot. "Now do Derrick." The command rasped out. And thank god she obeyed, because he needed the reprieve.

She smiled up at them, licking her lips, then turned where she knelt and took Derrick's cock between her lips.

"Yeah, baby, just like that," Derrick said as he pushed his hands through her hair, gripping a handful at the back of her head.

Now he got it—why his buddy was willing to share her, some of her, anyway. Because watching Hanna suck dick was fucking erotic as hell. Jeremy's hand slid up and down his cock in time with Hanna's rhythm. And Christ, he could almost feel her mouth on his shaft.

"You want her mouth back, man?"

"After I bury my face between her legs and make her come."

Derrick's gaze shifted to Hanna's ass as she crawled across the floor to the bed. "I'd say she's good with that plan." He moved to the side of the bed and angled his cock lower, toward her face where she'd turned it, her cheek pressed to the mattress. "This gonna work for you, baby?" He waited for her nod, then slid his cock into her mouth again. "Can't wait 'til you come. Fucking love it when you come with my dick in your mouth."

Jeremy's cue to get to it. With pleasure. He'd been thinking about this since his brief taste this afternoon. He slid between her thighs, looped them over his shoulders and took one long swipe with his tongue. Fuck it, he couldn't do slow right now. He plunged in, licking, sucking, goddamn devouring her. His cock had to be ten inches long. It banged against the end of the bed as he bored down on her clit.

She clutched the top of his head, pulling him in closer, harder. Her muffled moan mixed with Derrick's cursing. Her nails dug into his scalp. Her hips went wild, bucking beneath him as her spicy-sweet scent invaded his senses. Goddamn delicious.

"Have to do that again," he said as he lifted his head, "but not now."

"Fucking right, not now." Derrick's voice had the hoarse quality of a man who'd reached the limit of his restraint.

Jeremy knew the feeling.

* * *

"On your knees, beautiful." Derrick slapped her ass as she rolled, quickly obeying her husband's demand. "Time for the rest of your birthday present."

Hanna could barely think, barely breathe. Jeremy stood before her now, his thick cock awaiting her mouth, this time for full gratification. She didn't get to swallow often. Hot as the idea of it was, it always seemed like a waste. Because she loved it when Derrick came inside her, the sensation of his cock pulsing as he hit his peak. Tonight she'd have it all.

She closed her palm around Jeremy's cock and thumbed the bead from its tip. "Tell me when you're ready to come."

"You got it, sweetheart. I won't go too far."

"Such a gentleman. You need to stop that right now." She shook her head, letting her lips brush back and forth over the head of his cock as she did. "I want you to go all the way, but I want to make sure you're deep when it happens—I want every inch of your cock throbbing inside my mouth, I want to feel like I can't escape, like you own my mouth when you come down my throat."

"Christ…" was all he muttered as he pushed between her lips.

Derrick gripped her hips at the same time, and he thrust inside her body in a single motion. "Jesus, baby, I can feel every bump of that toy in your ass." He pulled back, thrust hard again. "Makes you so fucking tight."

God, yes, it did. But she couldn't answer, couldn't nod or signal. All she could do was take it, all of it — Jeremy's cock, fucking her face while Derrick's filled her pussy — and hope he found the button.

His hand branded her ass with a hard smack that sent heat searing through her core. He squeezed her flesh, ran his finger down the valley of her ass.

She moaned, desperate to tell him. She didn't need to.

"Fuck, do these —" The beads whirred to life inside her. Wiggling, vibrating, pushing her higher. "Oh fuck, they do. Jesus fucking Christ, baby…"

She fumbled until she found his hand, then dragged it to her clit. One touch from his fingers and she was on the edge. God, so much, so full.

"Gonna come, sweetheart…" Jeremy's voice as his cock thrust deeper into her mouth.

Derrick cupped the back of her head, pushing her onto Jeremy's cock. Holding her there. No escape, the way she craved it.

Their voices surrounded her, cursing and groaning. Their hands and cocks invaded her. Owning every inch of her, inside and out, as they came —

Jeremy, Derrick, her. No end and no beginning, just one tangle of erotic heaven.

"Morning, gorgeous." Derrick rubbed his beard against the back of her neck.

"Mmm..." was all she could manage after their incredibly late night. That and a smile as she wiggled backward, snugger inside the safe haven of his warm arms and hard body.

Make that *very* hard. The average adult male might wake up with morning wood, but Derrick's cock was better described as morning steel. Every. Single. Day.

After fucking well into the wee hours, though, her body needed a reprieve from that steely goodness. She wiggled again, this time in reverse. Somehow, she managed to escape the snare of his arms.

"Hey, I'm not done with you, birthday girl."

"The party's over for now, sexy husband. I'm a little tender in spots."

Derrick's face lost its playfulness. He abandoned the bed and had his arms around her before she reached the bathroom. "Want me to run you a bath, call the main building and see if they have any Epsom salts? I'll jet into town and get some if they don't. I can be back in twenty."

"It's not that dire." She cupped his jaw, ran her thumb and index fingers over his blond bristles. "But thank you for taking care of me."

"Never gonna stop doing that, baby." He dipped down to give her a soft kiss. "This okay, or are your lips a little tender too?" His devilish grin returned, accompanied by a wink. "They certainly got a lot of use last night."

She stuck her tongue out at him. "I'm going to take a nice, hot shower. Alone." Best to add that detail, just in case he had other ideas. "Take me into town for breakfast afterward?"

"You got it." He smacked her ass as she walked away, chuckling when she shrieked and scurried away. "What about Jer?" he asked before she finished closing the bathroom door. "Want him to join us?"

Did she? She'd decided in advance that once their fun ended, she wanted Jeremy to go to his cabin, not spend the night in theirs. Actually *sleeping* together seemed too intimate. Like kissing, the other thing she'd chosen to put on the no-no list. Things had been relaxed enough when Jeremy left last night, no awkwardness at all, in fact. She wasn't worried about what would happen when she saw him again because they'd already agreed — back to normal. She just wasn't ready for that brand of *normal* yet.

"No. I don't want him to join us. I only want you."

"Best words I ever heard."

God, his beautiful smile. Her heart flip-flopped and she fell in love with him all over again, for the ten-thousandth time. No need to say "I love you" — they'd both just done that. She blew him a kiss, closed the door and started the shower. Her reflection in the big mirror snagged her attention. She had some pink spots from last night, but it was her expression struck her first. She had the glow of a newlywed, or a lottery winner. Or a woman who, thanks to her amazing husband, had just had the best birthday ever.

Chapter Six

"Oh, damn it."

Derrick looked up from his bike magazine. A stack of colorful, paper apples sat in front of her on the coffee table. Shit. So did Hanna's overturned coffee cup.

"They're all ruined." The tip of her nose had already gone red. If he didn't intervene immediately, tears were the inevitable next step. She grabbed handfuls of the coffee-streaked apples and crumpled them in her fists. "I can't even make more because I used the last of my construction paper."

"So we'll get more —"

"I don't want to go back to the store. I don't want to have to elbow my way through a crowd of cranky parents and stand in a mile-long line. I just want everything done and ready for Tuesday."

He set the magazine aside and raised his hands in mock-surrender.

"God, I'm sorry."

"Don't be, baby. Beginning of the school year always stresses you out." He stood and moved behind her, kneading the knots in her shoulders with his thumbs. And yeah, copping a feel down her t-shirt, but hey. A man's gotta do what a man's gotta do. "Let me help."

"I'm unavailable for *help*, unfortunately. My stupid period came this morning."

Stupid indeed. How women dealt with that shit month after month, he'd never know. He leaned in, kissed the top of her head, swept her hair to one side and rubbed his beard against her neck. "That sucks, but it's not the kind of help I had in mind."

She tipped her head and gave him the "whatever" face. Understandable, since he hadn't been able to keep his hands off her for a single day since they got back from the resort. Some sort of caveman need to claim her every day, maybe. Not that she'd been complaining.

"So little faith in your husband," he said, pulling her to her feet and into his arms. "Here's what's we're gonna do to make things better. I'll clean this up while you change into jeans. Then I'm taking you for a long ride in the country that'll clear the crap out of your head. After I drop you back here, all nice and relaxed, I'll brave the wilds of Walmart on the last shopping day before school. I'll even help you cut out twenty new apples."

"How'd you know I need twenty?"

He tapped one ear. "Always listening, baby. Even when you think I'm not."

Her arms closed tightly around his waist as she melted against him. "You're too good to me—don't you dare ever stop."

"Ditto, baby."

Her eyes when she looked up at him nearly took him out at the knees. So much fucking love there. All for him. "Deal."

Shit, her car was gone. After the hellish day he'd had on the jobsite, Derrick didn't just want to see his wife, he needed to.

He turned his Yamaha into their driveway and under the carport he'd built a couple years ago. When they bought this place, Hanna hadn't yet landed a fulltime teaching position, and he was still low-man on the construction crew. A house with a real garage had been beyond their budget.

Hell, owning a house hadn't been in their budget. But he sure as fuck hadn't been willing to hear another snide remark from her mother about their one-bedroom apartment. The way Abigail Collins had said the words "rental unit" made it sound as if he'd forced Hanna to live in a box down by the river, eating scraps out of the overflowing garbage cans.

Hanna hadn't complained about the apartment. Not once, directly or otherwise. Like him, she'd been pretty damn happy there, because they were there together. She'd made that small space the best home he'd ever had. And she'd always defended it—and more importantly, defended him—to her mother. But he hated that she'd had to do it.

So he'd sold the classic Harley he'd spent years rebuilding and babying and slapped down a meager deposit on this house. Not that the aluminum-sided bungalow was anywhere good enough in Mrs. Collins' books. Nothing he did ever was. Kinda reminded of him of his old man. Only without the ass-kicking.

He stowed his helmet and gloves in the cupboard beside his bike, then headed into the house. He shucked his jacket but didn't remove his shoes. He'd figure out where she was and when she'd be back, then go for a ride. This house was a hell of a lot better than their old apartment, but without her presence, it was too damn quiet.

A paper hung from the refrigerator handle. Her perfect, teacher's printing reminded him it was open house night at her school. Leftover casserole in the fridge, home by eight and she loved him. A row of hearts, hugs and kisses completed the note.

Fuck eight o'clock. He needed her now. The rubber soles of his boots echoed as he retraced his route and left the empty house behind.

The school was in the upper-crust west end. A public school for children from wealthy families. Not the official motto, but it might as well be. The parking lot was packed with fancy cars and SUVs that looked as if they'd rolled off the line five minutes ago.

No sign of Jeremy's Hummer or Vivien's car. Maybe they weren't coming to meet-the-teacher night. Not as if they needed to—they'd both known Hanna for years. Derrick grunted as he dropped down to first gear. Jeremy in particular did not need a meet'n'greet with his son's teacher.

Derrick did a slow cruise of the school's lot and came up empty. One of the many advantages of a motorcycle over a car—the ability to make a parking spot out of next to no space. He rode over the grass to the tarmac portion of the schoolyard. His bike rumbled as he killed the motor, drawing disapproving looks from pretty much everybody within range, including a couple with a small boy in tow.

"Wow, cool," the kid said as they passed.

"No, Daniel. Dangerous." This from the dad, who walked as if he had a stick of raw ginger up his ass. Probably wondering which little shithead kid Derrick had spawned.

The mom, on the other hand, smiled. The kind of smile that said she wouldn't mind taking a ride on his bike...or him.

He shook his head, hung his helmet on his bike and followed the trio to the school. He quickened his pace before they reached the doors for the express purpose of holding it open for them. That seemed to burn the dad's ass more than the imaginary ginger up the dude's butt. Awesome.

"Thank you," the overly made-up blonde said.

Derrick nodded, keeping his eyes on the woman's face, even though she made no attempt to hide her examination and appreciation of his body. "Whose class is your boy in?" he asked, nodding at blondie's son.

"Mrs. Sutter's," the kid piped up. "She's the best."

Derrick smiled at the boy. "Yeah, she is."

"Oh, is your son or daughter in her class?" The woman's eyes widened as they all turned the corner toward the kindergarten rooms. Yeah, the wheels were definitely turning there.

"No, no kids. She's my wife." And with that little bomb-drop, they reached Mrs. Sutter's kindergarten room door. He slipped inside and out of the way, content to hang back and watch her do her thing, his constant hunger for her temporarily satisfied by the sound of her voice, the way her eyes lit up when she glanced his way.

Parents and little people continued to flow in and out of the room. He'd been in her classroom before, plenty of times the past few years. It was always bright and inviting. Homey. A place kids wanted to be, with a teacher who gave a shit about her students. He hoped they, and their parents, realized and appreciated their good fortune. The same kind he'd had when Linda Cruz was his teacher.

He'd been an average student on his best days. A sometimes troublemaker. But he'd never willing missed a day of school. School was sanctuary, a place Jim Sutter couldn't smack him around. He'd cheered along with the rest of the kids when they counted down to long weekends, Christmas or spring break and of course, summer vacation. But he'd fucking hated those times. Hated the extra time at home.

He looked around at Hanna's students. Scanned their small bodies and innocent faces for signs of trouble. None that he could see. Good. For the kids and for Hanna's sake.

"Hey, Luke, look who's here." Jeremy's voice cut through the haze of Derrick's reminiscing.

"Hiya, Uncle Derrick." Jeremy's boy bounded at him, wrapping his arms around Derrick's waist in the world's tiniest bear hug. "Aunt Hanna's my teacher, but I don't call her that at school. Well...sometimes I forget, but I don't get in trouble for it."

"'Course not, buddy. You're her favorite."

"That's what Mommy and Daddy say too."

Speaking of... He glanced at Vivien and Jeremy. Not looking any too cozy, but not looking as if they loathed each other, either. Basically, they looked like your average married couple with a kid.

Jer had gone to Japan on a business trip right after the night with Hanna, so he and Derrick hadn't been in touch a whole lot. Maybe he had reconciliation news. Much as Derrick wanted to rip a strip off Vivien for putting his buddy's heart in the grinder, he kinda hoped they were putting things back together. A good guy like Jeremy deserved to be happy. Having his family back would do that.

He'd have to catch up with Jer soon, get the lowdown. For now, somebody else required his attention. He crouched to Luke's level. "You like school so far?"

"I love it." Luke was positively beaming. "You and Aunt Hanna should have a baby. Then she could be his mommy *and* his teacher."

"*Luke.*" Vivien's fair skin now matched the big red crayon on the poster behind her. "I'm so sorry, Derrick."

"S'okay, Viv, no worries." He stood and offered his hand to the boy. "I'm gonna say hello and goodbye to your teacher. Want to come with me? I'll butt you to the front of that line of kids waiting to talk to her."

"We're supposed to wait nicely for our turn..."

"Rules are good, but sometimes you gotta break them, kid." He waved his empty hand once more. "You with me?"

Luke's small hand slid over his palm, the stubby fingers barely able to lace with his big, callused ones. "I'm with you. Let's do it."

The kid cracked him up. Behind him, Viv groaned and Jeremy laughed. Like old times. He led the way across the room, stopping directly in front of Hanna, much to the annoyance of everybody with better manners.

"Hi, Luke. I'm glad you came tonight." She'd bent at the waist, hands on her knees. She looked up and yes, totally caught Derrick gawking down the neck of her blouse. Cue the adorable headshake...yep, there it was. "There's a line, sir."

Sir, huh. He'd remind her of that later. For now, he grinned. "Yeah, saw it. I'm teaching Luke here to be assertive and go after what he wants." That actually got a chuckle from somebody in the line. Nice. "But if you want to give me a detention, I'll stay late and bang the dust off your brushes." The chuckler behind him appreciated that one too. As did Hanna, though she tamped down her amusement and issued him the *not here* face. Hint taken. "I'm gonna leave you to it now, Mrs. Sutter. See you at home." He gave his pint-sized accomplice a squeeze on the shoulder. "And I'll see you soon, buddy."

Aside from that quick exchange, he'd spent the last half hour in her classroom observing Hanna in teacher mode, not making out in the supply closet — an activity that was still on his bucket list. They'd have to do that before she bit the bullet and left teaching behind in favor of her other dream — social work. Even though he hadn't kissed her, had barely talked to her, he walked out of the building with a smile on his face. Seeing Hanna happy made everything right in his world. Made him think anything was possible.

He was sliding the chinstrap through the D-rings of his helmet when the hair on the back of his neck rose.

"You stupid little shit." A child's high-pitched cry followed the angry, male rasp.

The helmet thudded against the tarmac. Derrick did a quick scan and found the source of the noise. One row over, between the overpriced cars. Guy in a suit, steam practically shooting from his ears, and a cowering kid who couldn't have been more than eight or nine years old. Jesus.

"Look what you did." The guy grabbed the boy by the jaw and turned his face toward the open rear door of the car. "Had to bring that goddamn juice box along. You're as useless and uncoordinated as your idiot mother."

"Hey…" Derrick pounded his fist on the back of the car and stared the guy down. "You need to calm down and get your hand off that boy."

"You need to mind your own business." An abrupt shove forced the boy into the car. Sphincter-in-a-suit whipped the door closed, and the kid wailed again. Words barely discernible to Derrick, but clear to the douchebag dad, apparently. "Then move your ass when I tell you to get in the car."

Derrick stepped closer and looked in the window. Tears streamed down the boy's face as he rocked back and forth, cradling one hand with the other. "You slammed his fingers in the door, you piece of shit."

"He's fine. Get lost." He glared through the glass at his whimpering son and growled, "Shut up."

"You're done—I'm calling the cops," Derrick said, digging into his pocket for his cell.

"Fuck you," the asswipe said, then spat at him. *Spat.* The glob of spittle missed Derrick's face by an inch, landing on his shoulder instead.

Motherfucker had a death wish. "You should've dealt with the cops." The satisfying sound of cartilage popping filled his ears. Blood gushed from the guy's nose, but Derrick wasn't done with him. Not by a fucking longshot. "Now you're gonna deal with me…"

The guy issued another "Fuck you," then took a swing of his own, his fist grazing Derrick's jaw.

Derrick landed a second punch to the douchebag's face. For the boy in the car. For the boy *he* used to be. For his older brother, who'd taken extra abuse to lessen Derrick's whooping, many times. For all the kids like them, making themselves into tiny balls and hiding in musty boxes or piles of trash just to try to escape another beating at the hands of some monster they called "dad".

Voices flooded in, past the rage—the buzz of a crowd, a man yelling for Derrick step away. Hanna, calling his name.

He turned in what had to be slow motion. Saw her face, the one that'd smiled at him mere minutes ago, pale and streaked with tears. He blinked. Looked down at his bloody jacket and fists. At the man he'd knocked to the pavement.

Didn't matter that the scumbag deserved what he'd gotten. Only what Derrick had done. Beaten the shit out of another person with his bare hands. He'd become a monster. A typical Sutter male.

Fuck.

Hanna tugged Derrick's arm for the third time. She had to get him off the couch and out of the house. Break him out of this self-imposed prison. "I want to go out and have some fun. Come on, take me out."

"Not in the mood." His gaze remained glued to the TV screen. He shook her hand loose as if it were nothing more than an annoying fly that'd landed on his skin.

She'd let him stew for over a week. Enough already. "I know what this is about."

"Yeah, the game."

"Bullshit." Yup, that got his attention. And now that she had it, they were getting past all the broody crap. "You're afraid somebody from the school will see us."

"I don't give a flying fuck what anybody from your school thinks."

"More bullshit."

The corners of his mouth twitched. Getting there. He wanted to smile at the cursing, but he was trying to hold back. Guess she'd have to ramp it up a bit.

She hopped off the couch and planted herself directly in front of him, blocking his view of the TV. Of anything but her, actually. "If that's how you really feel, you won't mind turning off the goddamn game and taking your wife out for some bitchin' fun."

"Bitchin'?" He burst out laughing. "That's hardcore."

"You wait, I'm just getting started. You'll have to start a swear jar for me, just to get my mouth under control." She stomped one foot. "Oh snap. I guess I should've added some colorful adjectives in there."

He laughed hard enough to make him wheeze. "Baby," he reached out and pulled her onto his lap, "I don't deserve you." His beard rasped her neck. Warm breath from a long, low sigh tickled her skin. "And you don't deserve the shitstorm I caused."

Men — so frustrating. She cupped his jaw and lifted his face. "If you'd taken the time to listen to me over the past week, instead of attempting to become one with this couch, you'd know the storm died before it got started."

"I'm not welcome on school property again. Your weasel of a principal made sure I was clear on that."

"But there were no charges."

"Yeah. I kinda wish the prick had pressed charges." His jaw clenched beneath her fingers. "I'm free, but that kid is still trapped. If the cops had gotten involved, they'd have been obligated to investigate what I witnessed. You know that wasn't the first time the douchebag tossed his boy around."

So he *had* been listening when she gave daily updates. There'd been a reason Jon Whittle hadn't wanted anybody to call the police that evening. Whittle had a record of his own — well, almost. He'd twice been arrested for domestic assault, but both times, his wife had recanted her statement at the last minute. That much had been in the news.

"All of his teachers will be watching, now more than ever. We're trying to get him to open up to us."

Derrick snorted. "Good luck with that. As long as that kid's living with his dad, fear's gonna keep his mouth locked down."

Tightness tugged from deep in her chest. Derrick had been physically free of his father's heavy hand for many years, but not psychologically and emotionally. Maybe he never would be. All she could do for him was to keep the ghosts at bay by focusing on the present. The good stuff.

She switched to a straddle position and rocked her hips front to back. "I've missed you this week." She breathed the words against his lips. "Come back to me, please."

"It's not some switch I can flip."

"I know you feel bad, but—"

"Bad." A gruff laugh that had nothing to do with amusement rumbled between them. "I beat the shit out of a man, Hanna. In front of his kid. I'm not as smart as your family or your teacher friends, but you can dig a little deeper than your kindergarten vocabulary for this one."

And they were back to that nonsense. "No, I'm done talking." She pushed off his lap, grabbed up the remote and clicked the TV off with as much oomph possible. "Get up. I want to go out with my husband. And don't give me any blah-blah-blah about the game, because I'm going to be a wonderful wife and compromise — we'll go to JT's Roadhouse and sit in the bar so I can gorge on loaded potato skins and you can stare at their blinding array of big screens."

This time, his chuckle came with a smile. Not a huge one, but genuine. "Got it all figured out, huh?" He leaned forward, cupped her ass and pulled her to him, an action that put his face in very close proximity to parts he hadn't visited once this week, thanks to his mood. "What about later, you have a plan for that too?"

"I do." She sucked in a quick breath when his mouth closed over the seam of her jeans and his tongue pressed the hard ridge of fabric against her clit. "I'm tired of masturbating — I need you to make me come, I need to get fucked. Tonight. I'm done waiting."

"If that's what you need…" He stood, angled her head to his liking and sealed his mouth over hers for a long, slow kiss. "Then I promise that's what you'll get."

The last month had flown by. The business trip to Japan had eaten up two full weeks. The remaining time had been equally busy. Sixty-hour work weeks hadn't left Jeremy much time with Luke — a fact that had frustrated the hell out of him and massively pissed Viv off. His impromptu appearance on her doorstep the night of Luke's classroom open house had smoothed things over somewhat, though not enough to make her flexible about their weekend custody arrangements. That left him with a wide-open weekend that he'd rather have spent with his son.

It also left him with too much time to think about Luke's teacher. Seeing Hanna wasn't his motivation for wrestling his schedule into submission to free up meet-the-teacher night. Not his primary motivation, anyway. He should really use this free weekend to get laid. Get the memory of Hanna out of his system.

A female bartender stopped in front of him, nodding to her right once she had his attention. "The blonde at the end of the bar asked what you were drinking so she could buy you one. I told her I'd have to check." She smirked. "Figured I'd give you a chance to change your order to something more exciting than plain orange juice."

Jeremy looked toward his potential drinking partner. Early-thirties probably, pretty face with full, bright-pink lips, low-cut top filled that emphasized her ample cleavage. She waved at him—and blew him a kiss.

"She looks like a sure thing to me. So, what'll it be, handsome?"

The first legit smile he'd had in weeks made itself at home on his face. The blonde "sure thing" had nothing on the woman standing in front of him. Tall, with long hair that included several colors from the rainbow. A nose ring. Not the type he normally went for, but after that night with Derrick and Hanna, what the hell was normal?

He took a swallow of juice and shook his head. "Tell her thanks, but no thanks."

"Huh." She leaned over the bar and picked up his left hand. "No ring. Status?"

"Divorced."

"Nice."

He chuckled. "How do you figure?"

"Well, it means you're probably not gay," one eyebrow rose, "unless that's the reason you got divorced."

"Nope."

She released his hand and picked up a cloth. Wiped the bar in a circular motion that made her tits jiggle in an unintentional yet wholly mesmerizing way. "Divorced means you've made that trek down the aisle, so you're obviously not afraid of commitment. That's a big deal for most women. A friggin' aphrodisiac."

"Are you one of those women?"

"Ha, nope. I can't even commit to a hair color." She motioned at his almost-empty glass. "Get you something else?"

The words, "your number, for later" didn't make it out of his mouth.

"He'll have a beer." Derrick's palm landed solidly on his shoulder. "Better yet, we'll have a pitcher, and my gorgeous wife'll have…"

"An iced tea," Hanna said, filling in the blank. "Thank you."

Derrick slid onto the neighboring stool and swiveled so they faced one another. "How's it going?"

Jeremy glanced to the left, at Hanna. A hell of a lot better now, that's how he was doing. "Same old, just a bigger pile. How're you doing?" Hanna had texted him a few times after the incident in the school parking lot, asking him to call Derrick. He'd tried, but his buddy hadn't said much beyond grunts and single words. Since he was out of the house and speaking in full sentences, things must've blown over. A very good thing.

"Getting there," Derrick said, pulling his wife between his legs.

The act brought Hanna's hand in contact with Jeremy's knee. Briefly, but the air around them charged. She was so close now. Wide-eyed, her lips parted the tiniest bit.

His cock swelled at the memory of what that mouth could do. The greedy hungriness of her moan while she sucked him, how her eyes had pinched closed when she came with him deep in her throat. Christ.

"Let's grab a table." Before he did something stupid, like reach out and touch her.

"Sure."

He and Derrick stood at the same time, the act wedging Hanna between them, once again.

"Oh...sorry," she said, yet her hand didn't stray from where it'd splayed over his abs.

A couple inches lower and she'd have discovered his attraction to her hadn't ended when he'd said goodbye at the resort. Not by a longshot. He stepped aside and met Derrick's eyes. Braced for the punch he rightly deserved. But it didn't come.

"Third period's starting, let's roll." Derrick nodded at a small, square table near the shitty, coin-operated pool table. Worst place to sit if you wanted to see the big screens. "Look good to you, Jer?" His eyebrows rose as he tilted his head in Hanna's direction.

Oh man. If this night was headed where he thought it was... "Looks perfect."

From the cheering, the home-team must have scored. They might even be winning now. Derrick had lost all track of the game the minute they sat at the table.

He hadn't planned to initiate another night that included Jeremy. A one-time thing, they'd all agreed. But fuck, the heat coming off Hanna when she'd been accidentally sandwiched between them had made him insta-hard. Watching her get off that night at the resort had been off-the-charts hot. No reason it couldn't happen again. She'd insisted he show her a good time tonight, so that's what she'd get.

He caught her hand when she set down her empty glass. She squeezed his fingers and smiled at him. "See? I told you going out would be fun."

"It's gonna get a lot more fun, baby." He brought her hand under the table and settled it over his fly. "Stroke it." Back and forth, her hand moved over the denim. He shook his head. "Really stroke it. Open the zipper and wrap your fingers around my dick. Do the same for Jer."

"But…"

Anybody looking at them might've mistaken her expression as the deer-in-the-headlights type. Derrick knew better. He saw the lust and excitement in her wide eyes and parted lips. The longing for him to take her places she wouldn't go on her own. And that's exactly what he'd do.

"Look at him, baby." When she turned her head to obey, he added, "Look in his eyes. He wants you to do it." Yeah, he was making assumptions. Well-founded ones. He was no genius, but he wasn't oblivious. "I want you to."

"Another pitcher and iced tea?" one of the servers asked.

Great fucking timing. "Nah, I think we're done here."

"We are?" Hanna's bottom lip stuck out far enough to give even the poutiest of her kindergarten students real competition in the boo-boo-lip department.

"Yeah, we're gonna go to The Pulse."

"Dancing?" And boom, the smile was back. If she bounced much more, they might have to tie her down so she didn't get away. Not a bad idea, actually.

But first, a little warm up. "How about it, Jer — you up for it? Bet it's been awhile since you carved up a dance floor."

"Way too long. Count me in."

Somewhere along the way beer had morphed into Jack'n'Coke. Then he'd added tequila shots. Many, all courtesy of Jeremy's credit card. At least the bullshit in his brain had finally taken a backseat.

He had no fucking idea what time it was or how long they'd been here. Couldn't even remember coming out onto the dance floor, where one pounding beat blended into the next. The music never stopped, and neither did Hanna. In front of him, bouncing and gyrating, smiling and singing. Rubbing those sweet tits and hot ass against him. Then against Jer. Back and forth, teasing the ever-living fuck out of them.

She yelled something at him, but the thumping bass swallowed it up. When he shook his head, she grabbed his hand, shoved it down her pants. Sign language. Hell yeah.

He pulled her in, put his mouth to her ear. "I want you naked and on your knees."

She grabbed his neck and hauled his mouth down. Teeth clashed and tongues pushed together. They had to go. Now.

"Jer." Nothing. *"Jer,"* he called again. Still no response. So fucking loud in here. He found Hanna's ear again. "Get Jer so we can get out of here."

She nodded. Turned. Put an arm around Jeremy and brought his head down to her level. Whatever she said, it worked. He took the lead, cutting a path out of the wall-to-wall bodies with Hanna in tow. She grabbed Derrick's hand and pulled him tight behind her. No complaints there.

They swerved through the crowd. Past bouncers and a lineup of people waiting to get inside the club Jeremy had convinced them to try. Out of town, less conspicuous. Always the smart one.

Always the designated driver too. All their years as friends and he'd only seen Jeremy drunk once, at his twenty-first birthday. Just wasn't his thing, he'd said after that. Must be nice to have had that luxury.

"Hey, you." Hanna twisted in the front passenger seat to smile back at him. "You're awfully quiet. No passing out, got it?"

He snorted. "Not a chance. Seasoned pro back here."

She blew him a kiss and disappeared behind the black leather seat. Spent the rest of the drive talking and laughing with Jeremy. Nothing too flirty or sexy, but the chemistry was there. A steady hum with the occasional crackle of electricity. Because of their other night together — or had it'd always been that way? Huh. Maybe he was fucking oblivious after all.

He must've zoned out, because the Hummer jerked to a stop in their driveway. Nobody spoke. Didn't need to—they all knew what would happen next. Somehow they made it from the vehicle and into the house. Keys clattered on the floor. Shoes tumbled and clothes disappeared.

"Gotta have you, baby. Every part of you." He scooped those perfect tits into his palms and sucked her rosebud nipples between his teeth, one then the other, 'til she had her leg wrapped around him, rocking against his hip.

He'd promised to make her come but this wasn't how it was happening. He dropped onto the couch, pulling her down with him. "Move up. Want you on my face." Not something he ever had to tell her twice—his hot fucking wife loved it this way. She crawled up his body and settled just above his shoulders and waited, the way he liked her to. "Fuck, you smell so good." He stuck his tongue out and wiggled it against her clit. "Ride me, baby. Fuck my face with that sweet pussy."

Down she came, thighs boxing his head, all that delicious Hanna heat pressed against his mouth. He closed his eyes and breathed her in. Licked and lapped and devoured. He cupped her ass. Gripped her hard and spread her open, as wide as he could get her on the couch. It'd have to do. He slid his hands up to her tits, but Jer had beaten him there. He watched Jeremy's fingers roll and tug her nipples. Watched Hanna arch toward him, eager for more.

"Please," she said, tilting her chin up.

"Since you asked so nicely…"

Above him, Hanna giggled. Then moaned, as Jeremy's cock slid between her lips. In and then in some more, she took every inch. She let Jer fuck her face, loving it as she rocked her pussy on *his* face. Soon it'd be his turn for her attention. He took one hand off her ass and reached for his dick. Fuck—not limp, but not definitely not hard. Maybe it was the view. Can't say he'd ever wanted this much up-close information about his best friend's junk.

He closed his eyes. Focused on Hanna. Her spicy-sweet taste, her breathing as she edged closer to coming. Oh yeah, that throaty hum with the little hitch, then the soft, desperate whimper. She was so fucking close now. Time to take her over. He dragged a single finger through her heat and pressed it against her ass. Breached her, pushed inside. She cried out. Writhed on top of him the way she always did, riding it out hard. If he had to die young, let it be this way—suffocation by delicious fucking pussy.

She scrambled off him, went to her knees on the other end of the couch. She looked over her shoulder at him. "Come fuck me like you promised. And you," she crooked a finger at Jeremy, "over here."

Jeremy was in front of her in two seconds, cock in hand. As eager for Hanna's mouth as she was to finish him off.

His turn. He stood—his cock didn't. Fuck. He wrapped his fist around it, stroked and tugged as he moved into position behind Hanna. Her sexy curves waited—his to do anything he wanted with. Pussy, ass, both, any way he chose to fuck her, she'd love it. He slipped his hand between her legs. Hot, wet heaven. He braced his cock on his palm. Eased forward. As soon as the tip got inside, the thing would balloon up to normal. Had to.

Didn't. "Shit. *Shit.*" He fell back, legs tangled with his wife's as he stared up at the ceiling.

"What?" Hanna spun. Looked down at him with lust-glazed eyes. At his face, then lower. "Oh… Is it—is it me?"

"No. Fuck no."

"Then I can help." She nudged his legs apart and settled between them, ass in the air. "I'll make you so hard it hurts."

A private saying of theirs. How many times had he told her she did that to him—hundreds, at least. Silky hair fanned over his stomach. Her head bobbed, though it didn't have far to go. Because nothing changed. He could barely feel her mouth on him. Fuck.

"Enough." What the hell? Sexiest woman in the world sucking his dick and he couldn't get hard. "Fuck."

"It's no big deal—"

"Like hell it's not." He pushed up, off the couch. Nearly fell on his face. Would've, if Jeremy hadn't stuck his arm out and caught him. Jeremy, whose dick had no issue standing tall. Thing was a fucking club. "Jesus." He shook his head. Bad idea, made the blood that wouldn't go to his cock rush to his head. "Fucking whiskey…fuck."

"I'm going to take off, let you two—"

"You're not going anywhere, not until you fuck Hanna."

"*What?*" Her eyes went wide, but it wasn't exactly a protest.

"You want it. You need it and he can give it to you, so…yeah." The pounding in his ears blurred whatever they said as he walked away. He stopped at the edge of the hall. Looked back at them. At her. The beautiful woman who'd do anything for him. Who'd done everything he wanted since the day they met. He'd done shit in return. Got between her and her parents. Hadn't given her the family of her own she'd always wanted. Made a huge fucking mess at her job that could've gotten him arrested. Now this. He'd made a promise earlier and he was gonna keep it.

One hand on the doorframe, he pointed at Jeremy. "You have condoms?"

"Christ, D…"

He snorted. Some argument. Yeah, he got it. "Do it. But be gone by morning."

Chapter Seven

"Hey, did I wake you?" Hanna whispered as Jeremy walked into the kitchen.

"Indirectly. I smelled your coffee."

"Well, I'd say I'm sorry, but I'm never sorry about coffee, so I'll say good morning instead."

"Good morning." Man, that smile. His buddy was a lucky man, waking up to that every day. Jeremy took the seat nearest the stove so they could talk quietly. And to be closer to Hanna, not that it mattered.

If anything more was going to happen between them, last night would've been the time. They'd had Derrick's permission to fuck. Hell, D had demanded it before disappearing behind a bedroom door. Jeremy had been tempted to test those waters. Numerous times throughout the night. They'd spent hours on the couch together, talking between periodic checks to make sure Derrick wasn't face-down in puddle of vomit.

And Christ, he'd wanted to kiss her. Even once, to see what'd happen.

But what he wanted didn't matter. Hanna loved her husband. She'd broken down after Derrick walked away. She blamed herself for making him go out when he'd wanted to stay home. For pushing him to move on when he wasn't ready. For letting him drink too much. For selfishly taking advantage of his offer to be with Jeremy.

He'd talked her down, but damn, he'd liked hearing the part about him. Especially when she admitted that she wouldn't have done the threesome thing with anybody else. He deserved a medal for holding back at that point.

"Hungry?" she asked, bumping the refrigerator door closed with her pajama-clad hip.

"Very." Just not for food, after the abrupt halt to last night's activities. Nothing a date with his right hand couldn't take care when he got home. The minute he walked through the door, probably. "But you must be exhausted from last night—how about I take over?"

Sunlight streamed through the window and glinted off her hair as she shook her head. "I'm good."

He winked. "Yeah, I know."

"*Jeremy.*"

"Sorry, didn't mean to say that out loud."

"I'm tempted to withhold this to punish you..." She waved a mug of steaming coffee in front of him. "Or make you beg for it, just for fun."

"I'm not above begging."

She gave him an eye-roll, but it came with a smile. "I have a feeling that could get loud and I don't want to wake Derrick."

"True." He accepted the mug she offered. Ignored the charge of electricity that shot up his arm and down to his cock when their fingers brushed. Time to focus on his best friend, not his best friend's wife. "How was he when you checked last?"

"Still out cold. Didn't even flinch when I poked at him." The smile disappeared from her pretty face. "At least I don't have to worry that he heard us last night."

"He's going to find out. Kind of inevitable."

"I know, I just don't want to pile anything else on him right now. You won't tell him, right?"

He made a zipper motion across his lips. "Tell him when you're ready — he won't hear anything from me." He ticked off the remaining months of the school year on his fingers. "Nine months to go. Excited?"

Her smile returned, cranked to maximum glow. "I've been happy the past few years, but now that I've decided to go for what I really want, I'm giddy."

* * *

Jesus.

Derrick pressed his forehead against the living room wall. Wasn't bad enough they'd used the free-to-fuck pass he'd issued in his completely fucked-up state, they had the nerve to sit in his kitchen the next morning, flirting and planning their future. One that included a baby. Guess they hadn't bothered with condoms last night.

His stomach rolled over for the fifth time since he'd dragged his half-dead ass out of bed. If he had even half his normal strength, Jer would be eating his front teeth for breakfast. And Hanna... Fuck. He wanted to hate her. Hate would be easier than — this.

Dishes clanked together, followed by a startled, "Oh..." from Hanna. Then her laugh, light as air. "You're lucky I'm still going to give it to you after that."

"I'd just take it if you didn't."

Chairs scraped across the kitchen floor. *Thud* — the sound of something landing on the kitchen table. Somebody's ass, probably.

A grunt from Jeremy, then, "Damn, that's good."

"Sshhh, not so loud."

Another low, appreciate sound, courtesy of his backstabbing best friend. "Sorry, can't help it. In heaven here."

"Derrick loves this too."

And now she was comparing them? Fuck this shit. He laid his fist to the wall, rattling stuff on both sides of the partition, and rounded the corner, into the kitchen. "That's it, I'm gonna be sick."

"Oh my god, Derrick…" Hanna sprang to her feet. Was on him in seconds. "Let me help. Use the sink if you need to throw up again."

He pushed his fingers against his throbbing temples. Fucking Jack Daniels had never wrecked him this badly before. Maybe it wasn't the JD. Maybe it was the tequila. Maybe it was the fucking everything.

"Here, lean on the counter. Or me. Want me to get you a bowl or help you to the washroom?" She rubbed his back. Smoothed his hair and beard, even though he smelled like shit and probably looked about the same.

"Not that kind of sick." Everywhere she touched him stung. Good and bad simultaneously, like a tattoo needle. He brushed her hands from his body. She'd left enough marks. "Don't."

"Okay." Slowly, she backed away. As far as their small kitchen allowed. "When did you get up, how do you feel?"

"Worried about how much I overheard and who I might punch this time?"

"What?" She stared at him, wide-eyed and blinking. Until he took a solid, sharp step in her direction. Then she flinched.

His wife was physically fucking scared of him.

Made sense though. A week ago, she'd watched him cave a man's face in. Last night she'd fucked his best friend and sometime in the near future — when she deemed him able to handle it — she was gonna drop breakup news. And pregnancy news.

Maybe he *was* going to puke. He curled his fingers around the edge of the counter. Holding himself up and back at the same time. "Told you this'd happen."

"What would happen?" she asked. Even managed to sound innocent about it.

"Me, being this way." He let go, staggered a couple steps. "You, regretting it."

Jeremy rose from his spot. "You should sit down, man. Have some water. Toast if your stomach can handle it."

Too fucking much. "That's how it's gonna be?" He nodded at their plates on the table. "I shared my wife with you, and you won't even share your eggs?" A month ago, a comment like that would've had them all laughing. Maybe stirred up some fun. Nobody was laughing now.

"Derrick, please." Her whispered plea cut the silence.

He met her eyes. Glassy, on the verge of tears. No fucking way he'd let her suck him in. Not this time. "I gotta get out of here." He got past Jeremy with a single shove. Hanna didn't make a move to stop him. Shouldn't surprise him, but it did.

Keys, jacket, boots, and gone. Cool autumn air hit him as he walked out the front door. Snapped him out of his fog.

Jeremy's Hummer sat in Hanna's spot under the carport. Because they'd left her Beetle at the restaurant — right. They'd planned to ride over on his bike today so she could pick it up. Jer could take her. Hell, he was probably *taking her* right now. On Derrick's goddamn kitchen table.

He slapped on his helmet, mounted his faithful baby and brought her roaring to life. Yeah, it was early, and yeah, it was Sunday. The neighbors would be pissed, but right now, he didn't give a rat's hairy ass. He backed out of the driveway less carefully than usual. If his handlebars happened to scratch the side of Jer's SUV, too bad.

On the street, he kicked it into gear. The door opening and a flash of pink snagged his eye. Hanna in her silky pajamas, crossing the lawn toward him, the fall breeze lifting all that gorgeous, dark hair and making her look like something from a dream. He didn't wait. Didn't wave. Just rolled on the throttle and jetted the hell out of there.

The rumble of Derrick's bike had never sounded sweeter. Loud as it was, her heart jackhammering against her ribcage was louder. Hanna held her breath—and waited. The front deadbolt *thunked* open. His footsteps in the front hall echoed through the quiet house, then the door closed and the lock clicked a second time. Thank god he was home. Safe. With her.

She stayed in bed, blinking into the darkness beyond the bedroom. The shuffle of fabric told her he'd walked past. Without stopping to peek inside, without any type of greeting. Light from the bathroom briefly filtered in through the doorway. It disappeared, replaced by the sound of water hitting the tiles. She could wait or she could go to him. He'd been gone all day and night, hadn't called or texted once in that time, despite her repeated attempts to reach him. Clearly, he didn't want to talk to her. And that was just too damn bad.

She threw off the covers and padded down the hall. The bathroom door didn't have a lock—they'd never needed one. She slipped inside, but he didn't acknowledge her. The silent treatment meant she had a journey ahead of her if she wanted whatever this was resolved before going to sleep. So be it. She knew the very real consequences one could suffer from going to bed angry—she'd seen them play out, up close and personal, between Derrick and his older brother.

They'd grown up suffering the same abuse. According to Derrick, Chris had gotten it worse than usual when he tried to get between his little brother and their father. The bond that had forged meant Chris had received a free pass on many things over the years. But not all. Not slapping his boy, Derrick's then-five-year-old nephew, across the face. Nobody got away with that in Derrick's presence.

They'd fought, verbally and physically. Derrick had returned his nephew to the boy's mother, swearing Chris would never see the boy, or him, again. That threat—or promise, whichever it was—had come true. Chris died in a car accident that night. After all they'd been through together, their last day had ended in mutual hatred that would never be resolved.

"Do you hate me?" she asked.

"No." He didn't look at her. Just stood under the spray, letting it hit him in the face and roll down his hard, naked body.

"Do you love me?"

He rolled his shoulders, placed his palms on the tiled wall and braced himself with locked arms. He turned his head, met her gaze through the glass door. "Yeah."

Too much tension lived in that single word. But it was a yes, and she'd take it. "I was worried about you."

"Don't waste your time."

"Oh, okay. Sure. I won't give it a second thought next time my husband storms out and disappears for sixteen hours." No answer. "Is this about last night?" At this, he grunted, the kind of angry grunt-laugh he made about stuff that disgusted him. Men and their stupid, enormous egos. "It was one time, no big deal. Forget it and move on."

"You gotta be fucking kidding me..." He shook his head and turned his back to her. "Not talking about this right now."

"Fine." She dropped her silky robe on the floor, pulled the curtain aside and stepped into the shower behind him. She smoothed her hands over his shoulders, down his beautifully inked arms. Then around front as she pressed her body against his back.

"What the fuck is this, Hanna?"

"Us not talking." She wrapped her fingers around his cock. A couple of strokes and it swelled to its usual, glorious size in her palm. She pushed her hips forward, suddenly desperate for more, harder, contact—the kind this position would never provide. "I love your body." His skin was warm and slick from the water. She licked his back, kissed and bit it while she worked him with her fist. More. She needed a whole lot more. "I need to be with you tonight."

"*Tonight.*" He coughed out another of those venomous grunts as he turned. Eyes that were usually clear and blue as a summer sky were dark and stormy.

His hand shot to the back of her neck. He gripped her hard, then slid his fingers into her hair, where he used a fistful to pull her head back. "You want me to fuck you?"

"More than anything."

"Then stop talking."

Yes, he was probably embarrassed and frustrated about how the whiskey had rendered him impotent last night. But to be *this* angry about it twenty-four hours later made no sense. Especially for a man with his virility and strength of character. But whatever he needed to do to get past it, she was in.

"If you don't want me to talk, I suggest you keep my mouth busy with other things."

There. The hint of a smile. Of *her* Derrick. His lips came down hard on hers, his tongue demanding entrance as his growl filled her mouth. That's all it took for her body to go pliant against his. She wrapped her arms around his neck, her leg around his hip. Let his possessive kiss sweep her away.

He bent and lifted her in one easy motion. She gasped as her back hit the wall, the zing of pain shooting from multiple points of contact with ceramic. He didn't stop or check if she was okay. Just pushed inside her, hard and fast, borderline aggressive.

He pinned her tighter against the wall, forcing her hips to spread wider. Better access for him to pound into her. Which he did, over and over, grunting in her ear with each thrust. His hand in her hair forced her head to tilt. His mouth moved lower, to the side of her neck. Heat streaked from the spot. Not a light nip, his teeth clamped around her skin. She cried out, tried to escape the burn, but he held her in place. Biting, sucking — owning her flesh.

"Please…"

"Told you no talking." He almost barked the words at her.

She could play that game too. "And I told you to keep my mouth busy."

Then he was out of her, away from her, though his hand remained tangled in her now-soaked hair. A not-so-gentle jerk brought her to her knees. "Then get busy."

"I win." She swirled her tongue around the ridge beneath his tip. Teased the head of his cock in and out of her mouth. "This is exactly what I wanted to do."

"Less talking, more sucking."

"You said 'less', not 'no'. I call that progress."

"How about I say, shut up and suck my dick. How's that for progress?" Harsh words, but his mean-guy act didn't scare her.

One of the things she was certain of in this world — Derrick would never physically hurt her. If he gave it to her hard or rough, it was because he knew she wanted it that way. He always knew. Always gave her what she needed.

But she knew him too. And it was her turn to give him what he needed. "How about I say, 'with pleasure'." She opened wider and took him all the way, the insistent hum of desire between her legs ratcheting higher when the head of his cock bumped the back of her throat.

"Always gotta have the last word." His fist tightened in her hair, but his voice had lost its edge.

"Mmm-hmm…"   She   hummed   the acknowledgement while letting him slide completely free of her mouth. "And the last words are I love you."

God, his eyes, staring down at her. So conflicted.

She wrapped her arms around him. Scored his hamstrings and taut butt with her nails, eased one hand between his legs to give his balls the same treatment. She hummed again while looking up at him. Words he couldn't possibly understand, yet he did. His free hand settled around the base of his cock, holding it steady so she could fuck her mouth onto it, deep and fast. Water rolled into her eyes. Up her nose. She pinched her eyes closed and focused on breathing. Giving him everything she had.

"Fuck, baby, that's good."

That one word made her heart soar. *Baby.* As long as he called her that, they were okay.

She followed the river rolling down the crack of his ass and pressed one finger against his rim. A little breach, enough to hit some nerve endings and make him thrust into her mouth involuntarily. The only thing better than Derrick controlling the scene was Derrick losing control. With her, because of her.

His cock swelled, pulsed against her tongue, the inside of her cheeks. So thick and hot. She sucked hard as she let him slide from her mouth. She swirled her tongue under the ridge of his broad, deep-red cock head, then back and forth along the slit, lapping greedily at the beads of pre-cum.

"I love the way you taste," she said, then took him deep again, kept him there as she teased the tip of her finger in and out of his ass. His ragged breathing and muttered curses drove her higher. She hummed around his cock, stared up at him, pleading with her eyes, begging him to come down her throat—that sweet mix of losing and taking control she craved from him.

"No, not like this." The shower door banged open. He scooped her up, made the trip to their bedroom in a blink. He hit the lights and dropped onto his back, with her straddling his hips, her hands flat on his chest. "This way. So I can watch you move, see your face, feel you come around me."

Didn't matter that he'd been inside her thousands of times, including minutes ago. The sweet intensity of his words and voice, the gentle slowness with which he pulled her onto his cock, made tears well in her eyes.

He reached up to wipe one from her cheek. "S'okay, baby, I get it."

Got what? That none of the other stuff mattered if she didn't have him—not family or her job or lost wishes—he'd better understand that. She nodded, cradled his jaw between her palms and leaned in to kiss him. The only lips she'd kissed in a decade, and the only lips she planned to kiss until the day she died.

He caressed the lines of her body. Tactile worship that both relaxed and aroused her. Magical and addictive, she'd never get enough of his hands on her skin. One palm slid behind her neck. Gentler this time. A soft touch didn't mean he owned her any less, though. Every brush of his lips and sweep of his tongue sent sparks racing through her body. His hand spanned her lower back. Each thrust seated him deep inside her, each roll of his hips teased her clit with more friction, pushing her higher, closer.

"More," she whispered between kisses.

He gripped her hips, pressed her down, opening her hips wider until she got all the exquisite contact she needed.

"God, Derrick..." She rocked her clit over his pelvis. Bucked and clung to him, barely able to catch a breath.

"That's it, baby. Use me."

She did. A million beautiful stars' worth. They exploded beneath her closed eyes, lit her up from the inside and left her plastered to his chest, panting and entirely sated.

His arms banded around her and he pressed his lips to her hair. "Want me to stay?"

"Of course I do." She mustered enough energy to lift her head. "Where else would I want you to be?"

Against her body, his shoulders shrugged. In front of her face, the clouds returned to his eyes. "The couch."

Even through their darkest times, she'd never relegated him to the couch. Last night had obviously affected him more than she thought. She smoothed her fingers over his beard and smiled at the involuntary sigh her touch caused in this badass, strong-willed man. "I want you beside me. Wrapped around me, all night long."

"Then that's where I'll be."

Not that she tended to be a Monday-hater, but this one had ticked away with excruciating slowness. The students hadn't noticed Hanna's impatience with the day, but Megan had picked up on it.

"Want me to dismiss the kids so you can get out and get home?" she asked when Hanna glanced at the classroom clock for about the twentieth time in as many minutes.

"Thanks, but it's fine. I can't sneak out early—there's always somebody waiting to talk to me about something." Such as a parent with legitimate questions or concerns, or the principal with some nonsensical idea designed to make him look good with the superintendent, not benefit the student community. She'd miss the kids when she left her job at the end of the year. Not the politics.

The three-thirty bell rang. Twenty tiny people lost any remaining focus they had and the end-of-day scramble began. The clearing of knee-high desks, packing of knapsacks that in some cases nearly outweighed the carrier. Shoes were changed and jackets zipped. Hanna unlocked the coatroom door that led to the secure kindergarten playground and smiled at the lucky people waiting to collect their precious charges. The usual faces stared back at her.

Plus one—Jeremy, taking Vivien's place for pickup duty today. And oh boy, did he have the attention of the ladies in attendance. Rightly so. Jeremy Cruz in black pinstripe suit pants and a smoky-gray dress shirt was a sight to behold. Good thing Megan was inside. She hadn't stopped hounding Hanna for details about the birthday threesome, and her radar was way too sharp.

Hanna dismissed the kids in alphabetical order. Jeremy came forward and took Luke's hand, then stepped off to one side. She hadn't spoken to him since Sunday morning when he'd dropped her at her car—an hour or so after Derrick had stormed out and she'd subsequently burst into tears. As he had Saturday night, Jeremy had hugged and calmed her, talking her off another emotional ledge. He'd texted her several times Sunday afternoon and evening, checking in. When she'd sent off a quick message to tell him Derrick had finally pulled into the driveway, he'd replied immediately, despite the late hour. He'd certainly earned his good-friend badge this weekend.

"Hey," he said, moving in close after the last child had been collected. "How are you?"

Such a great guy. And given *all* she now knew about him, she really questioned Vivien's sanity, divorcing this man. "I'm good."

"Just good?" His eyebrows rose. He'd obviously noticed the change in her smile.

"Okay, I'm better than good. Much better."

"Guess you and D got everything sorted out last night?"

"Not exactly…" God, if her smile got any bigger, her face might crack open. "But we made up. He'd already left for work when I woke up this morning, but I'm sure we'll get around to the talking part tonight. At some point."

"Daddy," Luke yanked on Jeremy's arm, "can I play on the climber while you talk?"

"Sure, buddy, if it's okay with your teacher." At Hanna's nod, Jeremy kissed his son's head and let him go, eyes full of pride and love as he watched the boy sprint away. Jeremy had always been hot, handsome and nice. Fatherhood had served to amplify those qualities. Tenfold, at least.

"Where's Viv?" she asked, dragging her brain back to safer territory.

"In Vancouver, doing wedding prep for her sister's insanely huge event. Flew out earlier today." He leaned on the brick building with one arm above his head. The position boxed her in slightly, and suddenly her nose—and head—were full of his cologne and underlying, masculine scent.

"And Luke's staying with you until she gets back?" She edged sideways a bit. Necessary breathing room.

"Yeah. Four nights with my boy. If I didn't think Viv would go ballistic, I'd keep him home and spend some of the days with him too."

Yup. If such a thing as a "hot dads" calendar existed, Jeremy could definitely be the centerfold. Even with his clothes on.

"I arranged my schedule so I don't have to go farther than Toronto for a few hours while I have him, but the company I'm consulting for texted while I was on my way home just now. I have an international conference call I have to join," he flicked his wrist to check his watch, "shit, in less than an hour."

"Hint taken, I'm happy to help."

"Was it that obvious?"

"Just a little." She winked. After all the hand-holding he'd performed on the weekend, she certainly owed him a favor or six. "I'll take Luke home with me and you can pick him up when you're done."

He shifted and poof, that breathing room she'd made—gone. To make matters worse, he gave her an earnest yet sexy smile. "Would it be too much to ask for you to come over instead? The call won't take long, and I'd really like him to get settled at my place."

"Of course, no problem." So much for her plan to hurry home, start Derrick's favorite meal and greet him wearing her frilly, white apron and a pair of stilettos. "Let me finish up in the classroom and I'll follow you home."

Well, fuck him.

Derrick sat on his parked bike, half a block down from Jeremy's swanky executive home. He watched Jeremy help Luke out of the backseat of the Hummer while Hanna waited at his side. Any one of them could've seen him sitting here if they'd turned their heads. But why would they? They expected him to be on a jobsite somewhere. Not stalking the two people he cared about most while they enjoyed a happy-family moment.

Hanna laughed at something. The sound carried on the afternoon air, hit him straight in the gut. And her face…damn, she was practically glowing.

Jeremy had it all—big house, prestigious job, cute kid—no way Derrick could compete with all that, especially when he'd seen their explosive sexual chemistry firsthand. He'd been an idiot today, thinking he had a shot at keeping her. That if he put in more effort, showed her how much he needed her, she'd choose him. Last night hadn't been makeup sex, it'd been goodbye sex. Of the tear-his-fucking-heart-out variety. The really shitty part was, he'd known it at the time. Then he'd woken with his beautiful wife cuddled in his arms. Stupid fucking hope had gotten the best of him.

So he'd cut out early today—which had taken some major swapping of favors with the guys on his crew—thinking he'd surprise Hanna when she left work. Give her flowers, kiss the shit out of her, tell her all the things he planned to do to her at home. But Jer had been there. And hadn't that looked fucking cozy.

Kinda like now. Jeremy unlocked the front door and ushered Hanna and Luke inside. It closed and they were gone. She was gone.

He reached down, unclipped one of the saddlebags and pulled out the cellophane-wrapped daisies. Not fancy or expensive, but her favorite. They reminded her of running through fields of them as a kid. They reminded *him* of the time they'd made love in a field full of white blooms—the day he'd shown her where he'd had her name tattooed on his chest. Over his heart.

He glared at the bouquet in his hand, chucked them onto the street. Fuck the flowers. Fuck his stupid hope. And yeah, fuck Hanna and Jeremy too. He'd say they deserved each other, but the truth was, they did. They made a hell of a lot more sense together than he and Hanna did. So, most of all, fuck him.

Oh good, she'd made it home before Derrick. Dinner wouldn't be hot and on the table when he walked in the door, but *she* could be, and that'd do for starters. She dropped her bags in the front hall, kicked her shoes into the bedroom and hustled down the hall toward the bathroom, removing her clothes as she went. A shower would only take five-or-so minutes. She didn't need to wash her hair, but a fresh shave would be—

"In a hurry?"

She practically jumped out of her skin at the sound of his voice. "God, Derrick, you scared me."

He grunted. "That's what monsters do. We scare princesses." He was in his usual spot, the corner, one leg up on the chaise portion, the other bent at the knee, with his booted foot on the floor. A half-empty Jack Daniels bottle sat on the table. Cap off, no glass. The TV was off and he wasn't looking at her. Something really crappy must've happened to warrant this. Life certainly wasn't handing him a whole lot of breaks lately. At least she was home to smooth the rough edges.

"Good thing you're not a monster," she rounded the end of the sectional, "and I'm not a princess." The statement earned her another grunt. "Where's your bike?"

"Ditch. County road six, by the S-bend."

Oh god. She dropped onto the couch beside him, immediately checking for damage. "Are you okay — what happened, why were you out there in the middle of a weekday?"

He pushed her probing hands away, reached for the bottle, took a long swig and set it on his knee, fist curled around the long neck. "Looking for a goddamn willow tree, so I could wish myself back to the night we met. Want to know why, princess?" Venom tainted his ever-sexy rasp.

"Please don't call me princess."

"If the designer, glass slipper fits, princess, keep on fucking wearing it." He tipped his chin up and threw back a couple more ounces of whiskey. "C'mon, ask me why."

"Fine. Why are you drunk at six o'clock on a Monday night?"

"Not the right question, but it's the same answer for both." He jerked forward, got right in her face. "I wish I'd lost the coin toss that night."

"I don't know what that means, and right now I don't care. Tell me what happened today — what got you so stressed out you dumped the bike and proceeded to get drunk?" She slapped one hand over her mouth. "Oh no. It wasn't the other way around, was it? You weren't driving under the influence…"

"Fucking awesome. Not only am I an uneducated, lowly physical laborer with a violent temper, I'm a stupid-ass, doesn't-give-a-shit drunk driver."

"I don't think any of those things, Derrick. I never have." Enough. She'd get him closer to sober, then they'd talk about whatever had caused this. "I'm going to get you a glass of water and some food to absorb the alcohol."

He flat-out laughed at her attempt to pry the bottle from his fingers. "You're not gonna get it, princess. You only get what I want you to get, when I choose to give it to you."

"Stop being a dick and let me help you."

Darkness swept across his face. The bottle thudded on the living room carpet and he advanced on her, pushing her to her back with his looming physique. "Finally, a good idea." Metal jingled between them. His belt buckle, then his zipper. He shoved his pants down to his hips. "You can help my dick." He yanked her pants open. Had them off her body within seconds.

She sucked in a breath at the first thrust. The whiskey hadn't affected him this time—he was thick and hard as steel. He grunted and pushed deeper, the sensation of fullness reaching all the way to her womb.

"Gonna show you…" He growled as he pulled out, then slammed inside her again. "What a goodbye fuck," and again, harder, "really is."

"What are you talking about?" She shook her head side-to-side, desperate to see his face. The more she tried to make eye contact, the lower his face dropped. The deeper he burrowed inside and the angrier he growled against her skin.

His teeth clamped down on her neck. Heat streaked to her belly, and beyond. Then she wasn't overthinking, just wanting connection, whatever way he needed to make it.

"Derrick..." She shoved her hands down the back of his pants and dug her nails into his butt, pulling him closer.

But he didn't want that. He pulled out as fast as he'd started, flipped her to her stomach. One hand spanned her upper back, holding her flat against the couch. His other hand rested at the base of her spine. Then crept down, until his finger pressed against her rim. "I should fuck your ass one last time. So hard you never forget who owned it first."

One last time...more crazy talk that made no sense. It swirled in her head but she couldn't find words to argue. Not through the thick haze of wanting.

"Or maybe I'll just get your ass ready for his big, fat cock by stretching it with my fist while I fuck your pussy."

Who and what was he talking about...? She jerked forward at the invasion of his fingers, but his hand on her back held her in place. "No," she whispered, finding her voice.

"No what? No fucking your ass, or no filling it with my fist?" He punctuated the question by pushing his fingers inside.

It burned. God, it burned so good. "No one last time, no goodbye..." She moaned as his fingers twisted deeper, and panted out the remaining words, "Nobody's cock but yours."

"Got four fingers in you, baby, not a good time to lie to me."

Baby. Yes. "Not lying...please...don't stop. God, please don't stop."

He groaned and withdrew his fingers, leaving her empty and whimpering. Then he was draped over her back, his face in her hair as he slid inside her body. "I would've died for you, and now you're fucking killing me."

She couldn't breathe. Couldn't speak. From his mass on top of her, from his deep thrusts whooshing the air from her lungs. From his words.

He grunted as he came, then he was out, off and gone, stalking from the room.

"Don't you run out on me again." She scrambled after him, bracing herself in the kitchen doorway. "I won't let you."

He laughed—but it wasn't funny at all. "You couldn't stop me if you wanted to."

"*If* I wanted to? Of course I want to stop you. You belong here, with me."

"But you don't belong here, and you sure as hell don't belong with me."

"Why are you saying these horrible things?" Something was so, so wrong. She abandoned her post and went to him, even though his eyes shot daggers at her. He tensed under her touch, stared down at her with dark eyes as she traced the lines and swirls of ink from his wrists to the edges of his t-shirt sleeves.

"Don't," he said when she reached for his beard. He cuffed her wrists and pushed her away, his face shuttering as he crossed his arms over his chest.

"Why...I don't understand..."

"I won you in a fucking coin toss, Hanna. The night we met. If that quarter had landed the other way, you'd be barefoot and pregnant in Jeremy's kitchen right now, not secretly planning your escape from mine."

"My escape?" She clutched her head, shook it, squeezed her eyes closed. But when she opened them, nothing had changed. This wasn't some insane nightmare. Just reality that made no sense. "You flipped a coin for me?"

"Yeah. That's what we did when we both wanted to fuck the same chick. Feel special now, princess?"

Ten years together and he'd never told her. Neither of them had. She steadied herself against the table and met his narrowed eyes. He wanted her to be angry? No problem, she had that emotion covered. Just not for the reasons he had in mind.

"You think I'm that mindless? That your Neanderthal coin toss determined my future, not me?"

"I think you would've been just as happy to go home with Jer that night. Tell me that's not the truth."

"I don't know," she whispered.

"Bullshit. You're a lousy liar, princess."

"Because I'm not one, you son-of-a-bitch, and stop fucking calling me that!" She lunged at him, grabbing fistfuls of his t-shirt as she stared up at his face. "It doesn't matter what might've happened, only what *did* happen. I went home with you." She collapsed against him, wrapped her arms around his waist and let the tears roll. "I fell in love with you."

"And now you get to fix that mistake."

Chapter Eight

"You look like a zombie." Megan popped the last bite of her imitation-peanut-butter sandwich into her mouth. She chewed, swallowed, and washed it down with chocolate milk, then stuffed her containers back into her lunch bag. "And it's not the good kind of zombie, either."

Hanna groaned inwardly. Clearly she shouldn't have told her bestie how Derrick had nicknamed her "cock-zombie" because of her love of giving him oral sex. Or, greedily gobbling his dick, as he chose to describe it. *Used to* describe it. Since the madness that happened Monday after work, he hadn't spoken to her, not two words. Then again, it was hard to have any amount of conversation with somebody who didn't come home.

He'd been conspicuously absent every night. Staying out late, not answering her texts or calls, sleeping on the couch when he finally rolled in. The only thing that'd kept her marginally sane was his sobriety. No signs of staggering drunkness, no stench of alcohol. And he'd managed to get his bike back on the road. Time on his bike always helped to clear his head.

So she'd resigned herself to giving him space this week, hoping he'd wrestle his demons into submission and they could talk about things over the weekend. Starting tonight.

But she couldn't tell Megan any of this. Megan would just go into over-protective mode and hold a grudge against Derrick. Pointless, since Hanna was sure everything would be back to normal by the time Monday rolled around.

Hanna slid her purse straps over her shoulder and fell in step with her friend as they exited the staff room. "It's been a long week. The parking lot incident on open-house night dug up some old ghosts for Derrick. I'm doing what I can to be supportive while he works through it."

"Man, that sucks. Did you tell him that all the teachers and staff here secretly think he's a hero for pummeling that guy?"

"I tried. So far he hasn't been ready to hear it." Or anything else she needed to say.

Megan pulled her into a sideways, sort-of hug. "I feel bad for both of you. You should have told me sooner. I could've scalped my concert tickets and stayed in town to be with you this weekend."

"It's okay, but thanks."

"Maybe you guys should pretend it's your birthday and plan another special getaway weekend. You both seemed pretty relaxed after the last one..." She winked and issued a friendly pinch to Hanna's waist, then froze. "Oh honey, you should see your face...what's going on?"

Thank god for the bell and accompanying commotion. "That's us," Hanna said, turning away from her best friend. For the first time ever, she hoped the kids would be riotously bad all afternoon.

The sight of Derrick working on his bike under the carport felt like a lottery win. She'd left a note for him in the kitchen before turning in last night. It was still there when she got up, untouched, so she'd had her doubts he'd be here for dinner tonight. But he'd never been able to resist her crockpot stew. That old cliché about the way to a man's heart being through his stomach may have merit after all.

She gathered her purse and satchel and opened the car door. Speaking of stomachs—a thousand tiny butterflies had come alive in hers. A deep breath and a plan, that's what she needed. Okay, the plan. If he looked at her, she'd talk to him. No, scratch that sucky plan. She'd talk to him regardless. He was her husband, he had to interact with her eventually.

"Trouble with the bike?" she asked as she stepped out, onto the driveway.

He didn't get up from his hunched position, but he did make eye contact. "No trouble."

Well, he hadn't knocked himself out with that answer, but at least he'd answered. "That's good. I'm glad there was no major damage from Monday."

He grunted. "Yeah."

"Maybe you could take me for a ride this weekend—it's been weeks since I went out with you." Nothing, not even a nod or grunt this time. Great. "Unless you have other plans…"

"I do."

And the thousand tiny butterflies died in her stomach. But she wasn't giving up. "Well I *don't*, so I'll be around if you find yourself with free time and want somebody to hold down the back of your bike." More silence, with a side of stone-faced staring. "Did you see my note? I made the beef stew you like, the one with lots of big chunks of potato. I'm sure it's ready, if you want to come in and have some."

He stared at her for an incredibly long ten seconds. "Sure. In a few. Thanks."

Finally, a fledgling crumb of normalcy. "Great. I stopped for fresh sourdough bread to go with it, so I'll slice some up." On instinct, she leaned down and kissed him. A quick one that didn't require him to reciprocate. For now.

"Could you do me a favor?" he asked when she straightened.

"Anything. Always."

"You mind throwing my jeans in the washing machine when you get in there?"

"Not the kind of favor I was hoping you'd ask for, but sure." Could be wishful thinking on her part, but the hint of a smile seemed to play on his lips. She'd take it, no matter how small. "I'll see you inside."

"Hey, Hanna…"

She stopped with her hand on the doorknob and looked back at him. She would've preferred he call her 'baby', but her name was better than not speaking at all. "Yes?"

He opened his mouth, closed it and shook his head. "Nothing, forget it."

"You sure?" she asked, and he nodded. "Okay. We can talk in the house if you change your mind." She did a mini victory dance behind the closed door. Practically floated through the house as she collected his jeans and headed downstairs to the laundry room. Happy because her husband had asked her to wash his clothes—good god, she'd become a fifties housewife. She'd get him for this one day.

She flipped the lid on the washer and shook out the first pair of his jeans. Since she'd scooped them off the floor—and Derrick being Derrick—she checked all the pockets. A crumpled receipt and some coins. The next pair yielded a small wrench, a stubby screwdriver and a short pencil with lots of teeth marks. So typical. The floorboards creaked above her head. She hurried through the next round of pockets, stuffed them in the machine, then shoved her hand into the last pair. Two crinkly packages greeted her fingertips. Gum? He didn't usually chew gum.

She pulled them out and tossed them on the counter with the other pocket refugees. The blue squares stared up at her. "No..." She picked one up, turned it over in her hand. They'd quit using condoms the second she'd gone on the pill, almost a decade ago. These weren't his. Couldn't be. Please, god, they couldn't be.

Suddenly, somehow, she was at the top of the basement stairs. Then in the kitchen. Then standing in front of him with the condom packets in her hand while blood pounded in her temples.

"I found these in your jeans."

"Thanks," he said, plucking them from her between her fingers and shoving them in his front pocket.

"No..." Her legs buckled. She clutched his t-shirt and stared up at him. "Why—why do you have condoms?"

"Protection."

"Oh god..."

"Don't worry, I never fucked another person while we were sleeping in the same bed."

Which they hadn't done since Sunday night. "And since then?" Bile rose in her throat at his indifferent shrug. She swallowed it back, but nothing stopped the tears from rolling down her face. "You bastard."

"Told you I was. A long time ago."

Heat coursed through her. Her pulse thumped in her ears and a cyclone raged in her chest. She launched herself at him, balled fists landing on his chest. "Why did you do this to me? To us?"

He grunted. Oh god, no. It was a laugh. He was laughing at her.

"Betrayal is funny to you?"

"Not in the fucking slightest." His jaw clenched as he pushed her away.

"Tell me what you did." Nothing, he just stared. "Tell me, goddamn you!"

"I'm not telling you anything. You got a problem with that, you know where the door is."

Every muscle in her body shook. "Are you kicking me out?"

"I'm saying you're free to leave." He turned his back to her and lifted the lid from the crockpot.

The aroma of beef stew filled her nose. The rattle of dishes in an overhead cupboard echoed in her ears. She stood, frozen on the spot, as her husband—who had just admitted to cheating and suggested she leave—served himself a bowl of dinner.

He faced her again. Had the nerve to lean on the counter, bowl in hand, blowing on a spoonful of potato. As if this conversation meant nothing. What he'd done meant nothing.

"You owe me an explanation." She could barely choke out the words. Every muscle shook. And when he put the spoon in his mouth, rather than talk to her, try to fix this, something inside her snapped.

Suddenly she was in his space again. Rage like she'd never experienced welled up from her gut, set fire to her skin—skin covering a body she no longer controlled. Not consciously. She watched her hand knock his bowl to the floor, splattering food and shards of broken porcelain halfway across the kitchen. But the sensation didn't register in her fingers.

"Answer me." She heard the screamed demand. Her voice, yet she felt no hoarseness in her throat. And when all he did was shake his head and stare, she saw her arm rise, saw it swing toward his face, as if in slow motion.

She couldn't stop it. But when her palm connected with his cheek…the tingle shot down her arm, straight to her roiling stomach. "Oh god, Derrick, I'm s—"

"Get out."

She shook her head, not taking her eyes off of him, the horror of what she'd just done making her heart want to rip her chest open to be free of her. She couldn't leave. Wouldn't, until she fixed this, until they both did. "You can't force me out of my house," she whispered.

"We both know I could." He cupped her jaw, the touch of a man delivering a message, and stared into her eyes. "Leave. And don't look back."

The hammering at his front door roused Jeremy from his impromptu nap on the couch. He missed living with Luke, but the past few days had reminded him how much activity and attention a four-year-old boy required, and he was wiped from his stint as fulltime parent. He had to hand it to Viv, she did a great job with their son, and always had.

"Coming, hang on," he called when the second round of knocking started up. Probably neighborhood kids wanting a ball that'd gone over the fence into his backyard. Happened all the time, and they usually got it themselves, but he'd forgotten to unlock the side gate after Luke went home. The thought stopped him short. This house wasn't his son's home. *Viv* was home, no matter where she lived. Jeremy had become somebody to visit. Fuck.

He pulled the door open without checking the peephole. One look at her and he was wide awake, head to toe. "Hanna." Red-faced with smudged makeup ringing her eyes, she stood so close to the doorway, she was practically inside already. "Christ, get in here." He cupped her elbow and ushered her the remaining distance, closing the door behind her. "Did something happen with Derrick?"

She nodded, and the tears rolled immediately. "Oh god, it was horrible, and Megan's away and I can't go to my parents' like this—I didn't know where else to go, I'm sorry."

"Sshhh, it's okay, sshhh..." The smallest pull and she was plastered against his chest, her arms hugging his waist tight. He stroked her hair. Ran one hand up and down her back until her sobbing slowed enough to allow talking. "What happened?"

"Monday, when I got home from helping you with Luke, Derrick was already at the house. He'd dumped his bike and gotten drunk. He—" A large sob rippled through her and she shook her head against his shirt.

"He what, Hanna?" He spoke softly, but the heat had started to build in his gut. "Tell me what he did."

"He—he said cruel things to me, about me. Involving you."

"What else?" Because he damn well knew there was more to the story.

Her head shook again, as if she'd read his mind but refused to answer. "He didn't talk to me after that. Didn't text, didn't come home until he knew I'd be asleep. All week. Then tonight…"

This shit had been going for days and she hadn't reached out. Probably because he'd had Luke here. Shit. "Tell me. All of it."

"He was talking to me tonight. Not like normal, but talking. He asked me to wash a load of his jeans—"

"Are you kidding me?" He backed up a step so he could look at her. "After being a dick all week he asked you to do his laundry? What an ass."

"I found condoms in his pocket."

"Fucking Christ." He blew out a breath, tried to regroup, for her sake. "And you asked him about them, I assume."

"He thanked me and took them from my hand. He *thanked* me! Then he told me he'd never fucked anybody else while we were sleeping together, which we haven't done since Sunday night."

"And that's when you left?"

She shook her head, bit into her quivering bottom lip. "I tried to get him to talk, to explain why…but he wouldn't." Another sob rippled through her body. "I hit him."

"Oh shit." His best friend had come from violence, and had vowed he'd never live with violence again. It was the reason Derrick had refused to have kids—he didn't trust his temper, or his nature, as he insisted it was. The bastard deserved Hanna's wrath for what he'd done, but she couldn't have chosen a worse reaction. "Hit him how?"

"I slapped him."

A small mercy. At least she hadn't punched him or kneed him in the balls. "What happened after that?"

"He—" She started shaking, so much he could see her vibrating on the spot.

"He *what*, Hanna?" Must've been bad, because she just stared and shook her head, over and over. "Did he—" Fuck, he hated to ask. To think it could've happened. "Did he hurt you?"

"No. Not physically. But he hates me, Jeremy. He kicked me out, told me never to come back. Oh god, what am I going to do?"

"I'll go talk to him."

"No." Then she was on him again, arms wrapped around his neck like a vise. "That'll make it worse."

"How the fuck is that possible at this point?"

"Because he already thinks I'd be with you, married, barefoot and perpetually pregnant, if you'd won the coin toss."

Oh hell. Derrick had sworn him to secrecy about that little detail many years ago. The second D had realized he was head over heels for Hanna—which was about two days after they'd met.

Jeremy closed his arms around her. She relaxed against him, because of his touch. This whole situation was fucked-up. Including the fact that part of him saw this disaster as a second chance. He should ignore that part and step back. Let her cry on his shoulder, then head over to Derrick's and get the other side of the story. Try to help his friends with their problems. Not make them worse.

"I think…" Her voice hitched as she whispered, "I think it might be over."

There went the stepping back idea. Right out the front door. "You wouldn't be perpetually pregnant if I'd won that night, but there'd be a lot of practicing." He slid one hand up, into her hair. The other headed south, palming the curve of her ass, cupping it and pulling her tighter.

"Jeremy…"

If that was a protest, it was a damn weak one. Her soft voice and the fingers curled around the back of his neck were evidence of that.

"Derrick told you about the coin toss, but here's something he didn't tell you—I hated walking away. I'd never wanted to win one of those tosses more than I did that night, and afterward, I kept hoping he'd screw up so I'd get my shot."

Her heart hammered between them. Her warm, shallow breaths tickled the skin at the base of his neck. She tilted her head and looked up at him with those bottomless eyes. "For how long?"

"'Til I met Viv." At Hanna's wedding, of all places.

"Viv was a fool to divorce you."

"And Derrick's the biggest idiot on the planet, letting you go."

For a minute, she just stared at him. "Why didn't you say anything or let me know somehow—before the white dress and Viv, I mean?"

"Derrick was my best friend, I wanted him to be happy. God knows he deserved some happiness. And as I got to know you, I wanted you to be happy too. I still want that for you."

"Oh, Jeremy…"

"Sweetheart," he cupped the back of her head and brought her closer, "either push me away, or I'm taking my shot." He waited. No push. Deep down, he knew this was a scumbag move — for multiple reasons. At the moment, he didn't give a shit.

The full lips that'd worked magic on his cock were tentative under his mouth. But soft, so goddamn soft. He kept the kiss light, moved slowly, grazing her top lip, then the bottom, one corner and then the other. But Christ, slow might kill him.

He cupped her face. Brushed his thumbs over her face. "You're so beautiful, inside and out." No more warm-up kissing. He sealed his mouth over hers and she opened for him, an invitation he used to tease the tip of his tongue inside. So sweet, yet so hot.

He coiled his arm around her waist, holding her tight against him as he walked them through the house. Up the carpeted staircase, kissing and touching. Lips smacked together and their heavy breathing combined, the erotic mixture filling his head, making his cock hard as goddamn steel. Steel he couldn't wait to bury inside her sexy, writhing body.

He guided her to his room. She let out a little gasp when he scooped her into his arms. Another when he laid her out on the bed and covered her with the length of his body. He brought her hands above her head and laced their fingers together. Perfect, except for the band of warm metal his finger kept grazing.

"Jeremy, I…" She looked up at him, everything she thought and felt right there in those big, open eyes.

"I know, sweetheart." He dipped in for a short, sweet kiss, then pressed his forehead against hers. "I know."

The sight of Hanna flipping eggs and drinking coffee as if she did these things here, in this kitchen, every day, did things to Jeremy's gut. His presence in the entryway must have snagged in her peripheral vision, because her head jerked over her shoulder. And her smile—damn. How Derrick had given that up, Jeremy had no fucking idea.

He resisted the urge to puff out his bare chest when her eyes swept over it. But give her a raised eyebrow to let her know she'd been caught, oh yeah. "You're my guest, I should be cooking you breakfast, not the other way around."

"I'm more of a refugee than a guest, so I need to earn my keep. Plus, I like feeding people." She nodded toward the end of his granite-topped island. "Sit and be fed."

"I can do that." He slid onto one of the high-back stools, smiling when she passed him a mug of coffee. "Thanks." And by thanks, he meant, put down the carafe and sit on his lap. A mouthful of the hot brew kept the words from escaping.

She watched him, wide-eyed. "You're going to take a layer of skin off your tongue, chugging it that way."

"Worried I might damage it?" He winked and she laughed, then returned to creating breakfast sandwiches that had a hell of a lot more layers than his basic egg-slapped-on-dry-toast version. He took another sip, this one for pleasure rather than self-preservation. "Is this my coffee?"

"Sort of. I doctored it a bit. Like it?"

"Hell yes. Tastes like dirty dishwater when I make it." He chuckled at her animated wince. He set the mug down and stood, crossed the small gap between the island and the stove, between him and Hanna. "Now that you've shown me how good my formerly bland coffee can taste, you have two choices. Tell me your secret..." He lifted the spatula from her hand and set it aside. "Or stay and make coffee for me every morning."

"Jeremy, I—"

"Stop." He shook his head, an action that matched hers, but for different reasons. "Hear me out before you finish telling me no." He reached behind her, moved the pan from the stove and clicked off the element. "Come and sit," he said, leading her by the hand to the small sofa in the solarium part of the kitchen.

The robe she'd borrowed from his closet fell open when she sat, exposing her knees and the lower portion of her satiny thighs. She didn't fidget or try to fix it. Her eyes stayed on his face, her hands joined on her lap. Waiting to hear him out before she let him down. Only maybe she wouldn't.

"We've been friends a long time and probably know the good, the bad and the ugly about each other, in extreme detail."

Her soft laugh broke the tension. "That's a safe bet."

"Sure, knowing that you sound like a dying moose when you blow your nose takes away some of the mystique..."

"Jeremy!"

Christ, she was pretty when she blushed. "Okay, not a dying moose, more of a happy seal." He grinned as she jabbed him in the chest. "But it's a worthwhile tradeoff for all the other stuff. We're already good together, Hanna." He caught one of her hands and squeezed. "We could be genuinely happy, make each other's dreams come true. Not fantasies — real dreams."

"Derrick would never forgive you."

"Then I'll give him up." Hell, he already had. The second he'd kissed his best friend's wife.

"But I won't give him up," she said, pulling her hands away slowly. "The day might come when my heart doesn't feel like half of it is missing and the raw edge doesn't ache with every breath, but right now I can't begin to imagine that time. I don't want it to come because I don't want it to be over."

Yeah, he got that. A hell of a lot more than he'd like, thanks to Viv. He nodded. "Then stay and be my coffee wench. The pay's shit, but the benefits are pretty damn good." He finished by waggling his eyebrows exaggeratedly, which won him a smile. That's how she should always look, even if he wouldn't be the man to see it daily.

She hugged him, pressed her soft cheek to his chest, directly over his heart. "Were you heads or tails?"

Took him a sec, then it clicked. The coin toss. "Heads. Every time."

"Heads for the head lover, tails for the ass man." She laughed softly, but the warm, wet drops rolling down his chest told the rest of the story. "Part of me will always wonder what would've happened if the coin had landed heads-up."

"Me too, sweetheart." He buried his nose in her hair one more time. One last time. "Me too."

Derrick's cell vibrated on the asphalt beside him. He grabbed a rag to wipe his grease-streaked hands—

and thought of Hanna for about the thousandth time since her exit.

He'd ruined a lot of her clothes because he couldn't keep his filthy hands off her when she'd come out to watch him work on his bike or some other project. She'd never complained, but one day, the stack of neatly folded rags had silently appeared on a shelf near his tools. He'd preferred his solution—that she always be naked around him. Not so practical in a carport with the neighbor's window six feet away. They'd been socking away extra cash whenever possible to upgrade to a house with a garage in a couple years, but, yeah.

The cell vibrated again, a reminder of the text that'd come in before he veered down memory lane. He knew better than to hope it'd be from Hanna. Next time he heard from her, it'd probably be via a lawyer.

His plan to cut her loose had worked like a fucking charm. He knew she'd never leave him while he was down. He'd had to make her believe he was fine. Better than fine—that he was on top of the fucking world and didn't need, or want, her around. It'd made him want to puke, making her think he'd cheated. Had to be done, though, so she could move on. Finally have the life she'd always wanted. The things he couldn't give her.

He cleared the lock screen and tapped the message icon. The blue dot sat next to Jeremy's name. No surprise there, Derrick had been waiting for some version of this since Friday evening.

The message read, *We need to talk.*

Four words nobody ever liked to hear. He tapped a reply and hit send. *So pick up a phone. Say what you have to say.*

Not good enough. Has to be in person.

Shit. Figured. *Whatever. When and where?*

My house. Now's good. Going out of town on business tomorrow. Want to settle things before I take off.

Fine by him. He had a few things he'd like to settle with Jer, frankly. He sent, *Be there in fifteen.* He shoved the cell in his pocket, pulled on his helmet and brought the bike roaring to life. Show time—again.

He made the turn onto Jeremy's street, eyes peeled for one thing only—Hanna's car. No sign of it in the driveway or parked at the curb. He wasn't about to relax or read too much into that. The Beetle could be behind the closed garage door. More likely, she'd gone out so she wouldn't have to see him. Good call on her part.

Jer met him at the door. Dressed in cutoff sweat pants and a baggy t-shirt, he hadn't shaved and dark circles shadowed his eyes. Dude kinda looked like shit.

"Rough weekend?"

"Worried about me, man?" Jer's buddy slap to his back had more force than usual—or necessary.

Derrick snorted, leaned on the back of a leather club chair and crossed his arms over his chest. "Nah, you always land on your feet. Or on my wife." And it was officially *on.*

"You gave up the right to call her that when you took your dick elsewhere."

Confirmation that Hanna had run straight over here Friday night. That the condoms he'd planted in his pocket and his lack of denial had convinced her he'd fucked around. He could still picture her face from that night. Shocked at first, then devastated. And angry. The image would probably haunt him forever.

"You told her about the coin toss," Jeremy said when Derrick remained silent. "Thanks for that. Gave me the perfect opportunity to tell her how I felt back then." He stepped closer, into Derrick's space. "And now."

Baiting him. He stood stone-still. Squeezed his fists into tighter, harder balls.

"All our lives, you've cut yourself up, called yourself stupid and not good for much, and I've always disagreed. You finally proved me wrong, man. One kiss and I was hooked. Only a stupid fucking prick would let Hanna go after tasting those lips, especially knowing how incredible the rest of the package is."

His blunt fingernails dug into his palms. He opened his fists, flexed his fingers as his pulse hammered at his temples. A jab to the center of Jer's smug fucking face would feel so good. "This why you called me over, to rub Hanna in my face? You only have her because I let you."

"You really think that?" At Derrick's silence, Jeremy's mocking laugh filled up the space. "You ignorant, self-obsessed asshole."

Adrenaline coursed through his veins, tempting him to take a swing, to wipe Jer's fancy fucking floors with his bloody fucking face. "We done here?"

"Not yet." Jeremy was either the bravest guy on earth, or the stupidest, because he took another step. "Can you smell her on me, where her head pressed against my shirt while I held her? Is it driving you crazy not knowing what we've done since she showed up on my doorstep Friday night?"

"You need to get out of my face. Now."

"Not until you ask the goddamn question."

Derrick tried to sidestep him, but the ballsy fucker matched his movement.

"Only two ways out of here, D, and both of them are through me."

Every cell in his body vibrated. *Hit him*, they demanded. *Crush him*. Inflict the pain, not take it. A mantra that had been beaten into him for years. He blinked, long and slow, drew a deep breath and clenched his fists. Got ready for it. "Did you fuck her?"

"Does it matter?"

"Jesus. You must really want a beating."

"Not really. Willing to take one, though, to prove a point."

"And what fucking point is that? That you're as stupid as I am?"

"Nobody's *that* stupid right now, D." This time, his buddy's laugh had a genuine ring.

The sound defused the ticking bomb inside him, and he dropped into a chair. "You're right. Fuck." He blew out a long breath, kicked his legs out and leaned back. "Where is she, anyway?"

Jeremy took the neighboring chair, adopting a similar, exhausted position. "Good question." At Derrick's *what the fuck* expression, he added, "I invited her to stay, in any capacity she wanted, and she turned me down. Left this morning."

"Guess there's no rush for me to beat the hell out of you."

"Yeah, because *that* was happening." Jeremy snorted and motioned at their current positions.

So Jer *had* made a move on Hanna this weekend. That part, he could live with, since he'd pushed her — almost literally — into Jer's arms, and bed. The two of them made sense in ways he and Hanna never had, and never could. The earlier stuff, though, that tab needed settling. If not with Jeremy's blood decorating his knuckles, some other way.

"What's going on with you?" Jeremy asked.

The question brought Derrick back to the moment. "Other than my wife leaving me and my best friend trying his damnedest to bag her for himself? Same old, same old."

"Hey now. Hanna didn't leave you, dumbass. You checked out of the relationship with your drinking, sulking and fucking around. As for me, yeah, I tried. Which you expected, if not wanted, me to do when you shunted her out of the house. And now you're in my living room, one second looking like you want to rip me apart, the next, looking like the sad, solemn kid I used to beg my mom to adopt so he didn't have to go home anymore."

Shit. He never could hide the ghosts from Jer. Or from Hanna.

"So I'll ask you again—what's going on?"

"I screwed up."

"Understatement of the year, man. Care to expand on that little gem?"

Spilling his guts to the man who'd slept with his wife. It'd be seriously fucked-up if that man wasn't Jer. Okay, it was still pretty fucked-up, just a special variety of fucked-up.

"We got back from the resort and everything was amazing. So close to perfect. I walked into her classroom on meet-the-teacher night and for a few minutes, I thought about taking it all the way. Making it one hundred percent perfect, the way she's always wanted. Getting the snip reversed. I stood there, watching her with all those little kids, and I was halfway to planning how I'd surprise her with the news."

Jeremy nodded, a series of long, slow bobs that reminded Derrick of one of those old, drinking bird toys with the top hat and long beak that'll keep dipping its head because of perpetual motion. "Then the parking lot shit happened."

"Yeah."

"And suddenly you decided that more threesome lovin' would be better than a loving family?"

"Jesus, you're a pain in my ass."

"Ditto, man, but here we are." Jeremy leaned forward, elbows on the arms of the chair with his fingers tented together in the space between. "You want her back?"

Easy answer. "Doesn't matter what I want."

"You're right, it doesn't. It matters what Hanna wants. And that's you. So pull your head out of your ass, nail your demons in a box, and practice groveling, man. After the shit you pulled, you owe her, big time."

"Why're you telling me this when I know you want her too?"

"Because Hanna's been in love with you every minute of the last ten years, and she doesn't want that to change."

Much as he wanted to leap from the chair and go find her, he wasn't quite finished here. "What about you—are you in love with her?"

The weight of the question hung between them for a good, long minute before Jeremy answered. "I care about her. And I won't lie, it would be very easy to fall in love with Hanna, but no, I'm not." He stood, offered a hand. "We good?"

"Yeah." He rose from his chair, shook Jer's hand, then pulled him into a hug. "We're good."

As they slapped and released, Jeremy said, "In that case, I've got one more thing to tell you. Something you should know if you're going to try and move forward, but she might not want to tell you."

"About the pregnancy." Saying the word made his throat raw. But he'd just keep saying it until it didn't. "Don't worry, I'll support any choice she makes. I'll be a good dad, or stepdad. Or whatever. I promise you."

"I have no idea what you're talking about, D."

"I heard the two of you in our kitchen. The morning after I told you to fuck her because I couldn't get it up."

"Still no clue what you're getting at."

Jesus. Jer was gonna make him spell it out? Fine. "She was glad I hadn't overheard the two of you the night before, and made you promise not to tell me about the big event happening in nine months – the thing that she's always wanted. This ringing the daddy-to-be bell for you?"

"Goddamn." A fucking light bulb might as well have clicked on over Jeremy's head. "I'm still not telling you what I promised to keep quiet about, but I'm sure she will if you stop acting like an ass and jumping to conclusions all over the place."

"So you used a condom?"

"No, because we didn't have sex. Not that night, not ever. That's what I thought you should know."

"Why do you think she wouldn't she want to tell me that?"

"You hurt her, D, badly. With your silence and your words, and then with your wayward dick. If she tells you we had sex, it'll be to repay some of that hurt, and you should damn well let her. But I wanted you to know the truth—we didn't."

"Thanks. For everything."

"Always, man." Jeremy pulled him into another hug, thumping him on the back with affectionate gusto. "Anything for my brother."

Chapter Nine

The house hadn't changed over the years. Somehow, his old man had maintained its "piece of shit" level and the place hadn't dropped into the "unfit for human occupancy" category. One of these years. Then the walls that'd muffled so many cries and screams would have to be bulldozed to the ground. And what a fucking happy day that would be.

Derrick got off the bike and hung his helmet on one side. He hadn't been here since the day he escaped. Had vowed then never to set foot on Jim Sutter's property again, despite his dad's numerous messages asking Derrick to stop by since Chris' death. Now here he was. Before he could go to Hanna, beg forgiveness for his mistakes and ask for another chance, he had to do this. Go back to where it began. Put the ghosts to rest.

The decaying wood porch creaked under his boots. He palmed the handle, then let it go, rapping on the edge of the ancient screen door instead. Not his house to walk into anymore.

The inner door swung open and his old man came into view. It'd been four years since Derrick had seen him at the funeral, but from his appearance, it could've been fourteen. The skin on his face hung loosely from his cheekbones and jaw, pale and deeply grooved. His eyes looked sunken and his once-blond hair, a Sutter family trait, was now an ashy-gray. The booze had caught up to him.

The resemblance between him and his dad had always been strong. If he hadn't already decided to quit drinking, this could've been him in about thirty years. He wouldn't end up like the man before him, not outwardly or in.

"Derrick, son, my god." The door slapped closed behind Jim as he stepped out onto the porch.

"Which god are you praying to today, Dad—Jack Daniels or Captain Morgan?"

"Neither, boy. Sober now, twenty-five months and six days."

Now that they were only a couple feet apart, Derrick sized him up further. Used-up as the man looked, he also looked different—less raw, with clearer eyes. The sobriety claim might be legit. "Why'd you quit?"

"You. Your brother. My grandson." Jim scrubbed a weathered hand under his eyes, then gestured toward the door. "Want to come in? I got pretty good at making coffee after the shaking and DTs stopped."

The offer, his dad's demeanor, seemed genuine. And he'd come here to put the past to rest, once and for all, but go in that house…he just couldn't do it. "Out here's good."

Jim nodded, and a teardrop slipped down his cheek—one his gnarled hand didn't get to fast enough.

"I've never seen you cry."

"Didn't let it happen back then. Chased away anything that'd make me sad or guilty with booze. Being drunk and angry was easier."

"Yeah, I remember." Heat rolled in his gut. "That's why I'm here."

Another weary nod from his dad. "Been hopin' this day would come. I gave up calling you, but I kept hopin'."

He wanted to say his piece and walk away, go to Hanna, restart his life. Maybe it was the out-of-character tears, or the way his old man's voice cracked. He sighed and stuffed his hands in his front pockets. Leaned on the porch post and prayed the whole structure didn't cave in on top of them. "I'm listening."

"I have it written out in the house. A three-page letter, if you'd like to see it." His shoulders slumped when Derrick remained motionless, didn't invite him to take his time and retrieve the letter. "I wrote down what I can remember, though I'm sure there's more I don't. I'm sorry for all of it, boy. I blamed so many things and people for my actions…but they were my fault, every horrible word and deed. I'm not askin' you to forgive me, I just want you to know I regret what I did. I'm sorry I hurt you and your brother. Sorry that he turned out like me and it killed him, after it drove the two of you apart. It don't mean much coming from me, I know, but I'm proud of you. You turned out real good."

Not so good lately, but he was gonna fix that—permanently. He nodded. After all that had happened, "thanks" didn't quite fit. "Yeah. Okay."

"I hope you believe me."

"You kinda beat the ability to blindly trust out of me years ago." Jesus, Jim nearly crumbled in front of him. Derrick didn't even know this man. "But I want to."

"That's more than I deserve, thank you."

"Sure. Yeah." Nothing about this moment matched the scenarios he'd imagined. The rage was missing, on both their parts. So was his desire to get the fuck away. "I'd like that letter to take with me. I don't know if I'll read it, but I'd like to have it."

Jim moved as if a fire had been lit under his feet. "I'll get it." He paused halfway through the door. Looked Derrick up and down, nodding as he did, then disappeared inside the house.

Derrick pushed off from the post. He paced the deteriorating porch. What the hell was going on? He'd come here for closure, not this other shit popping up in his head. In his fucking heart.

He turned at the sound of the door banging closed for the third time. His face must've held one hell of an expression, because his dad froze on the spot, one arm extended, folded papers in his shaking hand. Jim Sutter was afraid of him.

As a kid, Derrick had dreamed of this day. Played it out in his head, over and over, multiple versions. The thought that someday he'd mete out payback was the only thing that kept him sane sometimes. Now was his chance.

He took the letter, turned it over in his hands a couple times before sticking it in his pocket. "This place could use some TLC…replace the floor boards that are rotting, install a new closer on that door to stop it from slamming against the frame." Jesus, this was nuts. "I could swing by with my tools and supplies, start on some repairs."

"Repairs." Jim's mouth quivered as he said the word — the old man hadn't missed its secondary intent. "That sounds real good, son."

"Yeah." He crossed the porch and made his way down the stairs, staying out of physical reach of his dad as he passed. No handshake or physical contact, not yet. Maybe one day. Hell, even that possibility was amazing. He nodded as he mounted his bike. "You didn't ask why I came over."

"Guess I was afraid of the answer."

No doubt. "I came to forgive you, put the past behind me for good, even if you were still a disgusting, drunk son-of-a-bitch." He pulled on his helmet, turned the key and pulled in the clutch. "I'll call you soon about those repairs." He pressed the ignition switch and headed east. Toward Hanna, the future, and the biggest repair job of his life.

Hanna was in the middle of *not* reading the book in her hand when Megan's doorbell rang.

"Pizza's here," Megan said, checking her watch as she sprang off the other end of the couch. "That was crazy fast. If the delivery guy's cute, maybe I'll give him a special tip." She winked while cupping her boobs through a skintight, white t-shirt.

Hanna shook her head, but she did it while smiling. "Should I make myself scarce? Give me a code word, so I can duck out the back door if I hear it."

"You're in an apartment, honey, no back door. But you're small enough, you can probably squeeze into the bottom of the linen closet." She stopped with one hand on the doorknob and wiggled her eyebrows in the most ridiculously exaggerated manner. "Ooh, or you could join in…"

"Oh my god, just get the pizza, you nut."

"I'm crushed." She fake-sniffled, then pressed her eye to the peephole. "Good lord, you have *got* to be kidding me. Honey, it's not the pizza guy, it's Derrick."

Predictably, her heart practically catapulted from her chest. After his recent behavior, she should want to throttle him, not have this desperate need to run to the door, throw her arms around him and never let go. "I'll talk to him."

"I knew you'd say that," the deadbolt clicked under Megan's hand, "but I'm talking first." Her friend's petite frame seemed to puff up to fill the doorframe. She pointed at him, her index finger poised within eye-poking distance, should the need or opportunity arise. "*You* are the king of douchebags."

"King's a bit harsh. More like sergeant-at-arms."

"Whatever. What're you doing here?"

"I need to talk to Hanna." He leaned against the frame, managing to look relaxed and charming, despite the fury rolling off Megan. His eyes lifted and locked on Hanna, where she clung to the couch cushions as if they were life preservers. "Please, baby, give me an hour."

Baby. With that one word, he'd bought himself the time. She nodded and rose, the action drawing a worried frown from her bestie, and a sweet, irresistible smile from her husband. "Let me grab my purse."

"And a jacket. We're taking the bike." He must've read her mind, because he added, "I brought your helmet."

"Presumptuous and cocky, what a surprise," Megan said, still not allowing him one inch inside the apartment.

"Safety-minded and hopeful."

Megan scowled at him, grabbed Hanna by the shoulders as she tried to slip past. "Honey. Remember all the things he's done. Don't let him take advantage of your soft soul anymore—he'll just hurt you again."

Before she could get a word out, in her defense or Derrick's, he jumped in.

"Megan, I appreciate you wanting to protect Hanna, I do. But she's willing to give me an hour, so maybe you could hold off on the insults until she hears me out. You don't want to wind up looking the dick friend who said too much if she decides to forgive me and take me back."

Oh god. He'd come to ask for another chance. And she wanted to give it. So, so badly. But she didn't need Megan's reminder. His recent activities had devastated her, and damaged them. Nothing that couldn't be repaired, but she wasn't about to roll over and absolve him. He had major explaining to do. Some begging wouldn't hurt, either.

Megan's hands slid away. "Be careful."

"I will," she said, directing the words at Derrick.

Megan's door clicked closed and the world shrunk in on them. He didn't crowd her, didn't touch her, but their connection was there, taut as a bowstring.

He smiled. A small one, the sincere kind. "Thanks for giving me a chance."

"I didn't agree to that. I said I'd give you an hour."

"Fair enough."

They took the stairs from Megan's second-floor apartment in silence. Derrick stayed close. Hanna knew without seeing that his hand hovered near the small of her back — it would've rested there, gentle yet protective, if things were normal. Their footsteps echoed in the low-rise building's small lobby. He pushed and held the exterior door, leaving her enough room to scoot beneath his outstretched arm, but not enough to pass without brushing against him.

"I missed you," he said as she squeezed by.

Traitorous, uncontrollable heart, it pounded hard against her ribs, demanding she simply jump into his arms. Instead, she lifted her chin and looked him in the eye. "Is this where you want to spend your hour talking?" Take that, heart. She'd stayed strong.

He smiled, reached for her hand and laced their fingers together. He brought her knuckles to his mouth, brushed his lips and beard against her skin. "Am I on the clock already?"

Damn him and his charming…everything. "I know what you're thinking, mister. A little kissing and rubbing equals magical, instant forgiveness. That's not how it's going to be. Don't mistake any smiles that might cross my lips—"

"Your gorgeous, sexy lips."

Damn him again. "Or anything you might see in my eyes—"

"Your hypnotizing, beautiful eyes."

She pulled her hand away and shook her head. "Stop it."

"Not gonna apologize for the truth."

"Then listen to mine. The emotions you see on my face are because I love you. I can't control the love, or I would've turned it off Friday night."

The flirty fun present in his eyes seconds earlier dimmed.

Good, he needed to understand. "The love is why I'm letting you take me somewhere to talk, but I'm not guaranteeing what happens after that."

"Got it. Sorry for taking liberties—hard not to when you're close to me. I missed you so fucking much, baby."

She nodded. If she tried to answer, her lips would undoubtedly betray her.

"I'm over there." He gestured to his bike, parked beside her car, and shrugged. "Yeah, the Bolt missed your Bug too."

The sight of his motorcycle with its gleaming, army-green tank and blacked-out exhaust gave her butterflies. Crazy that she'd missed his bike, yet she had. She sighed and slid her hand through the loop of his arm. A sucker, that's what he made her.

They walked without talking. He freed her helmet — the one she thought she'd never wear again — from its hold under a tied-down cargo net. Her hands shook as she fiddled with the chinstrap. She'd done this hundreds of times, in all kinds of situations and weather. Now though, the strap seemed twice as wide as the rings it needed to slip between.

"Stupid thing…"

"Here, let me." Gently, he tipped her chin up, got her buckled securely. "Ready?"

Ready to cry, throw up, maybe pass out — yes. The rest of her life was riding on the hour ahead. How could she possibly be ready for that? "I don't know."

"Then I'll walk you back to Megan's door and say goodnight."

God, now she really *was* going to cry. "You'd give up that easily?"

"No. Fuck no. I'll come back every goddamn day and try again. I won't ever give up, but I'm not gonna push you into something you're not ready for, not even a conversation. I already fucked up bad enough, baby. Not doing it again."

"I don't want to go back upstairs."

His thumb swept over her cheek, wiping away the renegade tear that'd escaped. "Then let's go."

She slid into place behind him, looped her arms around his waist and pressed her cheek to his back. The broken-in leather was soft and warm against her skin. She inhaled deeply, let its scent—one of Derrick's scents—fill her head.

She hugged him tighter when they began to move, closed her eyes and relaxed against him. The rhythm of the bike and the solidity of his body soothed her, as they always did. She didn't have to ask where they were going. Didn't have to look at their surroundings or pay attention to the turns he made. Her heart knew where he was taking her. Taking them. They were going home.

* * *

Another step accomplished. He had her on the back of his bike, heading to their house, and he'd do whatever it took to make sure this was a one-way trip. He'd given up on the idea of a higher power a long time ago—what god would let a child suffer the way he and Chris had—but right now he was willing to give praying a shot. If talking, praying and the gift he had lined up didn't work, well...he wasn't opposed to wife-napping. Instead of taking her back to Megan's apartment, he'd head for Niagara Falls. Get a room at that little motel where he'd proposed. Lock the door, close the blinds and wear her down in a dozen wicked ways. Maybe he'd do that anyway.

He pulled into their driveway, turned off the bike and waited for her to get off the back. She didn't. Didn't move a muscle. She wasn't melted against him anymore, either—her whole body had tensed up. And that was no fucking good.

"If the timer's going on my hour, I'm going to insist you slide your sweet little ass off the bike and go inside."

She sighed and got off, her small hands shaking as she worked the snap and buckles on her chinstrap. She managed it, though, and handed him the helmet.

He stowed both in the cupboard, watching her eyes go wide when he locked it, part of his "closing up shop for the night" routine.

"Like I told Megan, I'm hopeful." Oh yeah, there it was – the pretty smile he'd been stupid enough to think he could live without. He wanted to scoop her up and kiss that mouth so badly he ached. For now, he settled for her hand, squeezing it when she didn't pull away. "Come inside. Let me show you how hopeful I am."

"No guarantees, remember?"

"Who're you reminding, baby – me, or you?" A bit early in the game for teasing, but what the hell.

"Both." She untwined their fingers and leaned against the front of the house while he unlocked it. She stared at the open door, then at his face. "I need you to promise that once we're inside, you'll keep your hands to yourself."

"I promise."

"I mean it, Derrick."

Jesus, how was he supposed to keep a straight face when she used that adorable, schoolteacher tone that she truly believed worked on him the way it did on five-year-olds? "Yes, ma'am."

She slipped inside. Didn't take off her shoes or hang her jacket in the hall closet. Just walked through to the living room and perched on one end of the couch. As if she was a guest, not his wife of eight years and co-owner of this house and everything in it. Shit. Time to get serious.

Only she beat him to the job. "You cheated on me."

"I didn't. Not once, not in any way."

"How can you look me in the eye and say that after I found condoms in your pocket? Oh wait, I already know that answer to that—because we weren't sleeping in the same bed anymore. Only that wasn't my choice. You didn't give me a choice or a chance, you decided our fate on your own, then went out and cheated on me."

"You're right about not giving you a choice in my decision, but I promise you I didn't cheat."

"I can't believe you just did that…"

Jesus, her face. So pale, and the tears—shit. "Did what?"

"Used a promise to try to cover up a lie."

"I'm not covering up a lie. I did not cheat on you." More tears rolled down her cheeks. Fuck, not how this was supposed to go. "I'll prove it to you." A quick trip to their bedroom and he took the spot beside her. First thing he gave her was a box of tissue. Once she'd wiped the waterworks away, he handed her the second box.

"Oh my god, why would you give me this?"

"Count them." He pushed the condom box back into her hands when she shoved it away. "Dump them onto the couch and count them."

She tipped it, stared at the individual, blue squares that landed on the leather cushion. She didn't touch them. Instead, her eyes moved over the packets, silently tallying. "Twelve."

"How many come in that box?"

Her eyes darted to the discarded container. "Twelve..." All that beautiful, soft hair fell forward, hiding her face as she shook her head. "It doesn't prove anything—you could have replaced them," a big, single sob bubbled up, "or this could be a whole new box because you used all the other ones."

Shit, that hadn't even crossed his mind. "Look at me, baby." No change. "Please. I want to tuck your hair behind your ear and wipe your tears, but I promised not to touch you. Please look at me. Look in my eyes and know I'm telling you the truth."

Slowly, her face lifted. Hurt swirled in those beautiful amber eyes. All of it caused by him.

"The night we ran into Jer at JT's, I got utterly wasted, as you know." Bits and pieces of the wee hours had finally surfaced. How she—and Jer—had cleaned him up when he'd puked, several times. "But when I told him to fuck you, everything seemed so clear. Like it was happening outside of reality, but crystal clear. And it made some crazy kind of sense at the time. The next morning, when I overheard the two of you in the kitchen, I was sure you'd taken me up on the opportunity."

"I didn't."

"I know that now. But I was pretty messed up at the time." If only he'd talked to her about all of this weeks ago. What a fucking disaster. At least he had a chance to explain. To make it right. "Every time I closed my eyes, even to blink, I saw that douchebag lying on the pavement in the parking lot, staring up at me. Then it'd get all twisted and I'd see my dad looming over me while I was the one on the ground. I just wanted all the shit rolling around in my head to go away. So I kept drinking 'til it did."

She cupped her hands over her mouth. "I pushed you to go out that night—I should have known how deeply the school incident affected you, instead of thinking it was something my fun-loving husband could simply snap out of. I'm so sorry."

"Not your fault. We both know I'm capable of saying no to you, that I don't always give you what you want, even when you want it more than anything in the world." Which brought them back to the night everything changed. "Maybe I was still wasted the next morning, I don't know. But the stuff I heard…" He shook his head at his pigheaded stupidity. "I should've just barged in and asked what the fuck was going on. I thought you'd fucked Jer, and more than that, I thought you were planning to get together, permanently. I thought you were pregnant with his kid."

"Wow, his swimmers must've been pretty darn aggressive for me to know I was knocked up less than twelve hours later."

The sarcasm caught him off guard. Made him laugh. "Yeah, well, I'm no biology expert."

"I suppose that's true. You're more of an anatomy expert."

"Only yours, baby."

She leaned against the back of the couch and sighed. "Tell me the rest."

"My head was all over the place after that. I wanted you to choose me, stay with me."

"There was no choice, I've always wanted you."

"Not saying it made sense." He shrugged, shook his head. "I went to your school to surprise you with some daisies, was gonna plead my case. I was parked across the street, and I saw the two of you talking outside your classroom—it looked pretty damn cozy. I was convinced we were done. That you were holding off on breaking up until you thought I was more stable. So I decided to help you along. I acted like a total dick all week. But you didn't end it, didn't even call me out on my behavior. You just kept being all sweet and considerate. That's why I planted the condoms and made sure you found them. Almost didn't go through with it at the last minute."

"Why did you?"

He glanced at the ring on her finger—the one he'd given her for her birthday. "Remember on the beach? I told you if the day came when what we have isn't enough, I'd let you go."

"Oh, Derrick."

"I thought you were better off with Jeremy. That you wanted to be with him."

"And now, do you still think that?"

"Part of me's always going to think you'd be better off without me. I'm working on the broken parts, but I don't know if I'll ever be completely fixed." He scrubbed a hand over his beard and got a twinge of a smile when her eyes followed his fingers longingly. "As for the other part, I know it's me you want—or wanted, before I fucked up exponentially."

"I still want you," she whispered.

Best four words in the world. He leaned in, kissed her sweet, soft lips. She gasped, then sighed. Then moaned. He pulled back while he still had the power to do so. But damn, it about killed him.

"You promised no touching." Her tone chastised, but her glassy eyes indicated otherwise.

"Wrong," he nuzzled the side of her neck, "I promised to keep my hands to myself. I made no promises about my other body parts."

"Oh, I see…getting off on a technicality…"

"I'd rather get off on you." He worked his way lower, using his teeth to pull her jacket aside so he could nibble her tits through her t-shirt. "Inside you would be even better." He dropped to his knees and pushed between her legs. He made a show of clasping his hands behind his back—keeping his promise. He sealed his mouth over the bottom of her zipper, exhaling so she'd feel the heat through her jeans. So she'd squirm. "Right here, deep as I can get. But not yet."

"W-what?" She stared, open-mouthed and wide-eyed, as he returned to his feet.

"Not done trying to win you back." He stuffed his hands in his pockets and nodded toward the rear of the house. "C'mon. Next thing is out back."

She stood, tugged her little jacket back into place. "For the record, you were doing just fine on the couch."

A big old grin stretched his mouth wide as it could go. He hadn't smiled like this in weeks and damn, it felt good. But he couldn't assume things were on solid ground because of a little making out. They'd always had the physical part locked down. He had to be sure her head and heart were on the same track.

He paused at the back door and met Hanna's beautiful eyes. "Do you believe me about the condoms? Think about how I answered your questions that night—no admission or denial. I wish I hadn't hurt you that way, but I swear I never cheated."

"I believe you." She caught one of his hands and laced their fingers together, shrugging and smiling when he raised his eyebrows. "What? *I* didn't make a promise to keep *my* hands to myself."

"Not gonna complain about you touching me."

"Hmm...I think I may just take that as a challenge for later."

"You're staying."

"Well, duh."

His face actually fucking hurt from smiling. "I love you. I'm gonna spend every day of the rest of my life showing you how much."

"Start by showing me what's behind door number one. I'm dying to see how you planned to woo me in the backyard." She squeezed his hand. "Keeping in mind that I can't get arrested for indecent exposure, especially now that I'm going to be a social worker."

What the—

"Are you upset? I know we should have discussed the timing, made the decision together. I was going to surprise you with my acceptance letter from the university, but then—"

"Everything went to hell." Fuck the no-hands rule. He pulled her into the circle of his arms, where she belonged. "I'm sorry. And so proud of you, baby, always."

She looked up at him then. Eyes full of love and hope, the way they should always look. The way he'd make sure they stayed, from here out.

"I'm sure I can pick up a roster of tutoring clients that'll replace a chunk of my lost teaching salary, but when my tuition is due next fall, and with the textbooks I'll need, we're going to be hemorrhaging money for a couple years..."

"I don't give a shit about the money. We'll work out the finances part. It'll be fine. You'll be great." In the back of his brain, something clicked. "This is what you and Jer were talking about that morning. The thing you didn't want him to tell me. The big life change in nine months that was going to make you happier than you have been the past few years."

A big O formed on her lips. "That's why you thought I was pregnant..." She hugged him tighter and buried her face against his chest. "I stayed three years ago and I'm staying now. I wanted *you* ten years ago. It's *you* I want now. I wish you'd stop worrying about that."

He kissed the top of her head, kept his lips pressed there for a good long minute. "Speaking of wishes, let's go out back."

The temperature had dropped a few degrees and a cool, October breeze greeted them. It also rustled the boughs of the present he'd had delivered earlier.

"Oh my god, Derrick..." She fingered the delicate, trailing branches. Circled the pot where he'd set it on the deck. "You got me a wishing tree. I love it—I love you."

"It's a dwarf willow, but don't be afraid to wish big, baby. You'd be surprised what might come true."

Epilogue

The house couldn't get any cleaner or tidier. The scent of the mac'n'cheese casserole in the oven filled the kitchen. Hanna went room to room, doing one more visual sweep as she made her way to the front door. Everything looked perfect.

A beautiful May day greeted her when she stepped outside. Two male voices and clinking metal drifted from the carport. Wonderful sounds most of the time, but enough to send the butterflies in her stomach into fluttering overdrive at the moment. She cut across the lawn, ready to give them both what-for, until they came into view. Then it was all she could do to keep her heart from leaping out of her chest.

"Hey, baby," Derrick said, smiling and meeting her eyes. "What do you think—looks pretty awesome, right?"

"Derrick thinks it's ready to ride." Jamie looked over his shoulder at her from his seated position on the enduro bike. They'd spent the winter rebuilding it in the basement and had been tinkering with it out here since the moment spring arrived.

"Gonna take him over to the license office to write his beginner's test Monday after school—assuming he's finished his history essay by then."

"I will be."

Derrick clapped the boy on the shoulder. "Yeah, I know you will."

God, the two of them practically glowed. It'd been over a year since Jamie had come to live with them. Watching them together, it seemed as if they'd known each other forever. As though Jamie was Derrick's little brother, not a sixteen-year-old foster child.

She pulled a tissue from her pocket and dabbed the corners of her eyes. "Well, the bike looks great and I'm very excited about Monday, but I need you guys to wipe the grease off your hands—"

"Not on your jeans." Derrick threw Jamie a rag as the boy's hands moved toward his pants.

Good save by her husband. "Because Mrs. Benson and Michael will be here any minute and I want you to be able to shake hands." At that, Derrick and Jamie shook hands, both of them grinning like little boys who thought themselves very clever. She rolled her eyes at them, but couldn't help smiling.

She spotted Mrs. Benson's silver sedan as it turned the corner, onto their street. Derrick was at her side immediately, his strong arm wrapped around her shoulders, pulling her close. She leaned against him, absorbing his strength and warmth. His heartbeat thumped beneath her ear. Strong and steady, like the man, but faster than normal. A match for hers, currently beating wildly inside her chest.

The car rolled to a stop at the curb. Their caseworker got out first, waving at them as she walked around the vehicle.

"Ready to do this again?" Derrick spoke softly, for her ears only. He knew how hard it'd been to say goodbye to their other foster child when Brooke returned to her biological parents. But he also knew how happy it'd made her, seeing the joy in the little girl's eyes. Knowing she'd been part of that joy—that they both had.

The rear passenger door opened and Michael stepped out, onto the sidewalk. Not much joy on his small, pale face. Yet.

She smiled at the boy, then up at her husband. "I'm ready."

"Me too." This from Jamie, who'd materialized at her other side.

Together, they walked down the driveway, past the garden and the willow tree she and Derrick had planted two years ago.

"Making a wish?" he asked.

She shook her head. Smiled and squeezed his hand. "Nothing to wish for. Everything's perfect the way it is."

The End

Thank You!

Thank you for reading *Crossing the Line*! I hope you enjoyed Derrick, Hanna, and Jeremy's story. I would greatly appreciate you spreading the word, including leaving a review or star-rating wherever you enjoy discussing books.

Sincerely,

Karla Doyle

ABOUT THE AUTHOR

Karla is a small town girl with some big city experience, happiest living somewhere in between. She studied fashion design in college and spent most of her adult life in that industry. These days, she lives a charmed existence with her two amazing kids, an incredible (and smokin' hot) husband, and the best friends in the world. When she's not writing the sexy stories that swirl around in her head, you can find her lifting weights at the gym, playing Scrabble, or cuddled up with a book, surrounded by a pack of pets.

Visit Karla's website for her complete booklist and other information:
www.karladoyle.com

Connect with Karla on Social Media:
www.twitter.com/Karla_Doyle
www.facebook.com/KarlaDoyleAuthor

https://plus.google.com/+KarlaDoyleAuthor
www.pinterest.com/KarlaDoyleStuff

Send Karla an email at:
karla@karladoyle.com

Other Books by Karla Doyle

Cup of Sugar

Body of Work

More Than Words

Game Plan

An Excerpt from
Body of Work by Karla Doyle

Brian rolled to a stop on Sloane Street. He killed the engine and stared through the rain-covered window of his Jeep at the white bungalow. If he did this, if he knocked on Cassie's door at a quarter to one in the morning, there'd be no going back.

A man could only take so much. The petite brunette had caught his eye from day one. She'd been torturing him for months—chatting, teasing him with comments that made *her* blush, openly flirting with him while she exercised. He'd have made his move immediately if not for his stupid contract.

Which led him back to the decision at hand—to knock on her door or drive away?

He scooped the cell phone from the passenger seat. Weighed it in his palm and took another glance at her house. Light escaped around the edges of her closed curtains. If he didn't grab this opportunity, the odds of him getting another like it were slim. Fuck it, he was going for it.

Still raining and no sign it planned to let up. The drops cooled his skin, not the fire churning in his gut. He made short work of the distance to her door, each long step knotting his insides a little more. Yeah, he was nuts to do this. Nuts and committed to seeing it through. Worst-case scenario, she'd tell his boss and he'd get fired. Yeah, that'd suck—on multiple levels. He stopped a couple inches shy of the doorbell. Looked at the pink-covered phone in his hand and considered its owner. Her eyes, her smile, her body. The way everything inside him came alive when she laughed with him at the stupidest thing. Totally worth the risk.

He swallowed hard at the muted sound of the chime. Resisted the urge to press his face to the glass and look through the small window in her front door. Twenty seconds later, he rang again. Maybe she hadn't heard it. Or maybe she was hiding in a corner, waiting for him to leave. Another minute and he'd assume the second and haul his ass back to the car.

The outside lamp came on. Cassie's eyes popped into view in the lower portion of the window. They locked with his, instantly changing from a cautious squint to wide with surprise. The tip of her nose appeared, then her top lip. She had to be standing on her toes now. The rest of her mouth followed, curled in a smile. That's all it took—he was a goner for the thousandth time.

The thunk and scrape of metal as she unlocked the door ramped up the tension in his gut. When that door opened, things were going to change, one way or another.

Her soft voice and pretty eyes greeted him through a narrow crack. "Brian? What are you doing *here*?"

"You dropped your—" The door inched open. Wide open. Holy hell, there went his jaw, all the way to the ground. He'd seen Cassie in gym clothes and street clothes. Hot, sexy, adorable—those descriptions all fit, depending on the moment. Cassie in a silky, Oriental-patterned robe that barely reached the tops of her thighs and didn't close all that well in the front, wet hair framing her face…a word didn't exist to describe the sight. "You're dripping." Oh yeah, smooth opening statement right there.

"So are you." She giggled as a fat drop of water fell from his nose.

"It's really coming down."

"Thanks for the late-night weather update. Is that part of a membership upgrade?"

Messing with him now, was she? Exactly how he liked it. "Only for my favorite member." He pulled her cell from his pocket and offered it up. "You dropped this."

"Oh my god, where? I didn't even notice it was missing."

Restraint, he needed a bundle of it. In reaching for her phone, Cassie's robe gaped enough to give him one hell of a view. Add that to the charge that ran up his arm when their hands brushed and he nearly forgot the question. "Ladies' change room, near the lockers."

"How'd you know it was mine?"

He forced his eyes upward and—bam. Caught in the act of ogling her body. *Classy, man.* The door ought to be slamming in his face any second.

Instead, she waved the phone side-to-side. "Hmm?"

"I tapped the email icon. Didn't read anything, but I figured cassiebunny69 had to be you." The blush she got was unmistakable. "You might want to consider a passcode for your phone."

"Guess I got lucky that you found it, not somebody else."

Got lucky—his cock liked those words. At this point, his cock was a hell of a lot more optimistic than the rest of his soaked-to-the-skin self. "You going to the gym tomorrow?" A reasonable question to ask at one in the morning while standing in the pouring rain, right? Not too obvious.

"I'm not sure..." She turned the phone over and over in her hand. "Will you be there?"

"I will."

"What time?"

Time to play this out, see where it led. "Whenever you need a spotter."

"You're not working?" She stared up at him, pretty eyes getting bigger when he shook his head. "You want to...work out with me?"

"Actually, I want to do a hell of a lot more than work out with you, Cassie." Lightning cracked behind him and the street lost power. Fantastic timing, nature. He could barely make out Cassie's silhouette, let alone read her expression. For all he knew she was frozen in front of him, too scared to respond or make a move. "Go inside and lock the door. I'll see you at the gym sometime."

"Brian, wait..." A small, soft hand latched on to his arm. Pulled him closer, over the threshold, close enough to smell the shampoo she'd used and feel the waves of heat rippling from her freshly showered body. Close enough for him to make what could end up being a huge mistake.

Want to read more?

BODY OF WORK is available now.

An Excerpt from
More Than Words by Karla Doyle

Eight thirty. Shit, he was late. Travis tossed a handful of kibble in the cat's bowl, grabbed his guitar and jetted out of the apartment. He should have been at The Cove already. The guys were going to have a heyday with this one. Dependable Travis, last one to the gig for once. He could practically hear them now.

He needed something to shut them up. Not the truth. Hell no, if they found out he was late because he met a girl online, and worse, during a Scrabble game—he'd never live it down. Guys who played rock music didn't behave that way. They weren't supposed to behave at all.

The club's parking lot was overflowing when he pulled up. Excellent for his band, even though he had to park down a side street. Not only was Black Box getting the standard flat fee for the gig, they were getting a cut of the bar receipts during, and for an hour after, their set. Thanks to him. The guys never mocked his business savvy. That alone should be enough to keep his bandmates off his back. As if it would.

Fabricating some story was easy enough. The question he couldn't shake was why some faceless female on a geeky game site had gotten to him. Women threw themselves at him all the time—young ones, old ones, and an incredible amount of smoking-hot ones. Even small-time musicians got laid a lot, freely and without any expectation of commitment. A perk of the job, until it grew old. Now he couldn't stop thinking about C Ya, wondering exactly what she looked like, where she lived, if she walked around wearing lingerie just for the hell of being sexy. For all he knew, *she* wasn't even a she. He ought to give his fucking head a shake.

"Cat puked on my clothes," Travis said as he climbed onstage, past a bunch of raised eyebrows. "Nothing worse than a messy pussy." The crude joke got a laugh. He slipped the strap over his neck and started plucking and fine-tuning. The stage lights were still low, making the press of bodies visible if he looked up from his pearl-white Fender P Bass. If he'd pushed, maybe C would have told him her full name and where she lived. Between Toronto and London covered a lot of ground, and he was smack in the middle of it. If she lived close enough, he could have told her where he'd be playing, and…

Get real. Not only was she likely a monster to look at, but she probably lived in some hick-town hours away. And the whole point of chatting on that site was to avoid groupies, not make more. A woman who found him interesting for his brain, who wanted more than to ogle or idolize him, that was what he wanted. Well, that was mostly what he wanted. He'd be strumming another kind of instrument later tonight to take care of the rest.

The house lights dimmed. A rumble erupted from the crowd as the bar manager stepped onstage for the introduction.

"We're packed to capacity tonight, folks. If you don't have a drink yet, flag down one of our beauties and get a couple, because you're gonna need 'em. Our favorite homegrown boys are here to rock you into a hot, sweaty mess. Ladies, and the rest of you ugly lot, give it up for Black Box," he said, then jumped into the mash of patrons.

Applause, screaming, hooting. Travis' adrenaline spiked with the noise. He struck a chord and led the band into their first song, letting the sensations take him over. The neck of the guitar became an extension of his arm. Blood surged through his veins, into the frets, along the strings and back into his body, carrying his soul into the music and the music into his soul. The crowd was there—the electricity of them surrounded him—but he saw nothing. Two songs turned into five, then the bar manager was back, announcing their break.

The stage lights dimmed. Stubbs, their keyboard player, crouched at the edge of the stage. Talking to a woman, of course. Travis slung his guitar aside and sipped ice water, scanning the crowd through lowered eyes. Hundreds of bodies, tons of them women. If he wanted to hook up later, all he had to do was make eye contact with one of them. Or more than one. Been there, done that. Yah, being with more than one woman was hot, no denying that. But all of it had gotten so meaningless. Sex for the sake of getting off, nothing more.

Still, he found himself searching. Tons of women with long, dark hair. Any one of them could be his Scrabble mistress. Or none of them. He'd never know…unless they chatted again and she opened up. Maybe he'd get the ball rolling. Something about her made him want to take the risk.

Behind him, Luke plugged in his guitar and began playing a medley of riffs. Travis joined in, the lights came up and the crowd screeched approval. Not much topped that sound.

They ended the night's performance with the Guns N' Roses cover he'd mentioned to C. He usually went to a totally free place during his solo, but tonight he was thinking of her comment that it was a romantic song. He closed his eyes, tried to conjure an image of his mystery girl. If she was real, the flesh and blood kind of real, he'd play it for her. Acoustic, slowed down to make it sexier. And close up, so they could share the heat of it.

He very much needed to get a grip.

"Dude, come sit at the bar." Victor, Black Box's crazy-ass drummer, poked Travis in the ribs with his drumsticks after their last set had finished. "Bring your strings, chicks love that shit."

"Nah, I'm out of here, for which you should thank me, otherwise I'd steal all the best ones from under that hideous moustache of yours."

Victor laughed, smoothing his fingers over the bushy inverted horseshoe. "The ladies love it. They say it tickles them in all the right places."

"I'll try not to keep that in mind," Travis said as he walked away from Victor, endless free drinks and a sea of liquored-up, willing females.

King Street was wide awake at midnight. The mouth of the club was thick with bodies still waiting to get inside, even though the live music had ended. In his peripheral vision, the building appeared to have puked people onto the concrete. No doubt there'd be plenty of real vomit out there later. Thank god he was past all that.

Back home, he tossed his keys on the table, undressing as he walked through the apartment. He settled on the bed with his laptop, a bottle of water and Kersh — the roomie he'd inherited with the apartment, a black cat that refused to move out no matter how many times he left the door open. At least the place was mouse-free.

"Away from my goods," he said to the kneading feline, tossing the blanket over his lap to be safe. He logged on to the Wordloverz site and off just as quickly. Damn, she wasn't online. He grabbed the pad from the side table, reviewing the notes from their earlier chat. Not much to go on. The strongest clue was the slogan she'd quoted from her workplace. If the business existed, he'd find it. The internet was as much his home as the stage, paying his bills more consistently than his music did. He typed the tagline into the Google search bar. The store had to have a website—everything and everybody had a web presence these days. Hell, he had his share.

"No way." There it was, an independent business with the exact catchphrase. Here, half an hour from his place, less on a good day. The odds of that had to be miniscule. And she wasn't kidding when she told him they sold the works. Holy shit, it sold some sexy stuff. Critically speaking, the online store looked pretty good. Professional and easy to navigate, though there were places it could have been even better—and would have been, if he'd designed it.

He scrolled through the pages, past lingerie that went from church-lady reserved to porn-star racy, not stopping to look at anything specific until he got to the accessories area. Candles, oils, soaps, jewelry. Nice. Next came the hot stuff—sport sheets for bondage, role-playing get-up. Holy hell, there were a lot of choices. Vibrators, dildos, nipple clamps…and she'd sampled some of this stuff? The images that brought to mind.

It wasn't until Kersh pounced on the blanket that Travis realized more than his mind had wandered. He cursed the cat but couldn't blame him for misinterpreting the kind of playing going on beneath the covers. Yeah, he'd decided. For better or worse, he had to know, had to get a look at the naughty Scrabble vixen. Tomorrow he'd be taking a trip to Romance U.

Want to read more?

MORE THAN WORDS is now available.

An Excerpt from
Cup of Sugar by Karla Doyle

Well, look at that – Nia's little Chevy, its lights on, but not running. Perfect timing.

Conn pulled into his half of the joined driveway and parked beside her car. For the eight months since she'd moved in next door, the twenty-four feet of asphalt separating their houses had been almost impassable. Whenever he got close to crossing the distance, something or somebody got in the way. Overtime on the jobsite or a time-consuming sideline project he couldn't afford to pass up. Phone calls from his family that he had to answer. His pissed-off ex dropping by to unleash her rage. Yeah, that last one had particularly sucked.

The times he'd had the opportunity to speak to Nia, she'd blushed throughout their brief, casual conversations, bolting as soon as she had the chance. Polite, neighborly waving seemed to be her preferred method of communication.

But he'd caught her looking his way. Many times. The pretty blonde's ability to fry his circuits with her stolen glances had had Conn on high alert for months. Hell, he'd purposely put himself on display – doing all kinds of things – hoping she'd get tired of secretly watching and come knocking on his door. She never did.

He wasn't one for making New Year's resolutions, but this opportunity called for one. Tonight, he resolved that Nia wouldn't get away so easily.

He stepped onto the snow-covered ground. Not much accumulation yet, but the forecast called for six inches before the calendar rolled over at midnight.

He'd shovel it before it piled up, then again later, when it quit coming down. He'd do Nia's side of the driveway too, as he did whenever she didn't beat him to the job.

She was a petite thing, but never shied away from property maintenance. Such as climbing a ladder to clean out the eaves troughs—which she'd done wearing cut-off jean shorts and a pale-pink, body-hugging tank top. Best day in all of August, that one.

He left the shopping bags in the backseat of his truck and cut between their vehicles. The groceries could wait a few. Spotlights mounted on Nia's backyard pergola illuminated most of the driveway. She hadn't started her engine, nor had she gotten out of the car. Intentionally avoiding him? If so, about time he found out why.

He bent and peered through the window, giving a light rap on the glass as he did. "Hey, neighbor."

Her muffled "hello" was as soft as Conn imagined her skin and hair would be—if she ever let him close enough to find out. Her gloved hands gripped the hell out of the steering wheel. The keys dangled from the ignition. Small clouds formed and dissipated as she breathed the cold air. She darted another glance at him, but didn't move.

"Everything okay, Nia?"

Her shoulders slumped and a larger puff of fog left her lips. "My car won't start."

Chalk this one up as a late Christmas present from the universe. He motioned at the passenger door. She nodded in response, so he opened it, stuck his head and shoulders inside. "I'm at your service. I can jump you or give you a ride."

She squeaked — actually squeaked — and the frost melted from her expression. Oh, she was still pink in the cheeks, the color just didn't look cold-weather induced. Maybe this New Year's Eve wouldn't completely suck after all.

But he didn't grin, though it pained him greatly to hold it in. Any sign of wolfishness and she'd bolt again. That much he was pretty damn sure about. No problem. He could take it slow and easy.

"What happens when you try to start it up?"

"It goes *click click click click click.*"

Goddamn, she was cute. So much so, the grin almost got away from him. He nodded at the steering column. "Mind giving it a go so I can hear it? Not that I'm doubting the accuracy of your impression."

"Oh god, of course. Sure." She mumbled something under her breath while leaning forward to turn the key in the ignition. The Chevy clicked in rapid-fire succession.

"Okay, good enough. You can stop. I'm not a mechanic, but I'd wager it's your starter. Maybe the solenoid." A guess he'd already made, based on the operational status of the car's lights and the adorable-as-hell sound effects she'd made.

"What's a solenoid? Wait, better question — what are the odds I can get it fixed tonight?"

"Unless you have a mechanically inclined relative or close friend with access to automotive parts and a warm garage, I'd say zero."

"What if you jump me — will that help?"

It'd help him, hell yes. But he couldn't say that either. Not to a woman he didn't know beyond some casual conversation and eight months of ogling from his side of their mutual property line.

"Nope. That only works for a low battery. And yours," he nodded at the windshield, beyond which her headlights bounced off the fence, "seems to be working just fine."

"Shit." She slumped again. A cloud of curly fog rose as she sighed. "Thanks, Conn."

Since moving in, she'd never called him by name. And man, did it sound good in her sweet voice. If she thought he could close the car door and walk away after hearing that, she could think again.

"Give me ten minutes to toss my stuff in the house, feed Zeus and I'll give you a lift wherever you need to go."

She didn't raise her head, but turned it enough to look at him. A curtain of long, blonde hair obscured half her face. "Why?"

"Why not?"

The eye he could see squinted at him. "Because it's New Year's Eve and I'm *quite sure* you have plans."

Really now. This could get interesting. "And why would think that?" he asked while sliding onto her passenger seat and closing the door.

That move had her sitting straight. "What are you doing?"

"Being neighborly."

"Oh my god, just no." She shot from her seat and out of the car as if her cute little ass was on fire. When he didn't follow suit, she leaned in and scowled at him. "Are you going to get out?" She rolled her eyes and huffed at his shrug. "Good lord, this is all I need."

"See, now we're getting somewhere. Tell me what you need, Nia. A ride to…?"

"I do not need to ride you." Forget squeaking, this time she shrieked. Then clapped one gloved hand over her mouth, and with the other hand, slammed the driver's side door.

He choked down the gut-busting laugh that threatened at the base of his throat. But when she reached the door of her house and realized she'd left the keys in the ignition, the dam burst. One loud laugh erupted from his lips. No doubt that was going to get him in serious shit with his neighborette. He'd just have to make it up to her.

He removed the keys, locked her car, and headed toward her house. A steady flow of fat snowflakes filled the column of light surrounding her. Made her look like a Christmas angel. The innocent look—his weakness. And that weakness had bitten him in the ass more times than he cared to count.

A smart man would learn from past mistakes. Toss Nia the keys and back the hell away before he made another. Instead, his boots were clomping up her steps.

"You might need these," he said, pressing the keys to her palm.

"Thanks."

Not giving an inch, was she? All right. He leaned on the bricks, biting the inside of his cheek as she fumbled, twice dropping the keys onto the snow-covered deck. "Want some help?"

"I'm fine."

Indeed. "How about a *lift* somewhere," he winked, "since you're not interested in a ride."

She scowled at him, the teasing obviously missing its mark. "Fine. I was on my way to Barry's Bay to visit my parents. Go take care of your dog and I'll meet you at your truck. You should probably pack snacks, you've got a long trek ahead."

"Barry's Bay?"

"Yes. Do you know where Bancroft is?"

"Yeah." Fucking far away, that's where.

"Just a bit north of that." She shot him a smug smile. "Still feeling neighborly?"

If they drove non-stop at normal speed, they were probably looking at a six-hour drive. In this weather, he'd bet on seven, maybe eight. They wouldn't make it to their destination until well past midnight.

"Guess I have a date for New Year's Eve after all. See you in ten, neighbor."

Want to read more?

CUP OF SUGAR is now available.

An Excerpt from
Game Plan by Karla Doyle

Andie rose from her spot at the end of the front row bench and laid on the hooting and clapping. Her son looked over his shoulder and rolled his eyes. At twelve, Dylan rode the line of being glad for his mom's attention and wishing she'd blend into the crowd like *normal* mothers. As long as he still smiled at her antics, she wasn't about to give them up. This season, he remained her little boy.

And damn, the boy could hit. His worm-burning line drive zipped past the first baseman and found a home halfway into the outfield. Dylan rounded second, had a look, thought better of getting greedy and dove back to the bag. He'd be proud of those bruises tomorrow. Cheers and whistles filled the air as she watched her son brush dust off his knees. The noisy fans all but drowned out the warning she heard a second too late.

"Ow — what the?" She grabbed her ankle, hissing at the heat spreading above the bone. Everyone around her remained focused on the game. Nobody had noticed her crumple in pain. Not even Scott from across the diamond, even though he'd barely taken his eyes off her for five innings.

She eased onto the bench and rolled her leg sideways. A baseball-sized welt had already formed above her right ankle. The foot she used for sewing. Terrific.

"Hey, are you okay? I yelled over at you."

"Apparently you need to get a better set of lungs, because I didn't hear you." The snarky response left a bitter taste in her mouth. "Sorry, that's the pain talking, not me. I'm not always a bitch."

"No worries, I get it. Taking a hit stings. It's my fault anyway. I shouldn't have drilled the ball that hard on the sidelines. Here, lemme take a look at that ankle... Damn, it's rising faster than a twenty-year-old virgin getting a lap dance."

Andie's first thought was that the guy needed to shut up, there were kids nearby. Her head snapped up to tell him so and the thought fell away. Kneeling in front of her was what could only be defined as a prime candidate. Full head of light-brown hair with exactly the right amount of messy, incredible blue eyes and lips designed for making out. And since the buttons on his baseball shirt had been neglected, Andie was treated to a view of one spectacular naked chest.

"I take it back, your lungs look fine," she said, and clapped a hand over her mouth. Major slip of the internal thought process.

The hunk looked up at her, totally amused. "They do, do they?" He scooped her foot into his hands and placed it on his thigh as he examined her ankle.

Strong fingers gently but thoroughly traced over her flesh. Yes, he was merely checking for damage he might've caused. It was still the best contact she'd had in forever. Her own hands got the job done, but they didn't send a thrill through her system. Thank god she'd shaved her legs this morning. Not that he'd notice or care.

Andie's mind headed for the scenario he'd mentioned. Except she became the dancer, gyrating over the bulge in his lap. And he was no virgin. Uh-uh. In her version of the strip-club seduction, the athletic stud beneath her was a sexual MVP.

"It's not serious, but it needs to be iced." The deep richness of his voice yanked her out of the premium-grade fantasy. "You bring any ice packs?"

She swallowed and shook her head. No way could she speak to him again. Not after telling him his chest looked good, and especially not after picturing herself grinding onto his cock. God, her face must be beet red. The way he grinned—he had to know. Oh, but he was pretty. And much younger than her. Too young for her to be picturing naked and sweaty.

"I'll grab you some ice from my cooler." He sprinted away. Baseball pants had always been one of her favorite things about the game. On this guy, they were downright erotic.

Lasha slid in beside her. "Who in the name of tasty treats was that?"

"Just some guy who hit me with a ball. A case of being in the wrong place at the wrong time."

"Just some guy, huh?" Lasha raised an eyebrow. "So switch places with me. Maybe I'll get lucky and be in the wrong place too."

"You don't want one of these." Andie turned her leg so Lasha could see the now-monstrous bump.

"No, but I'll take one of those." Lasha nodded toward the pure testosterone jogging their way. "I wouldn't mind if he groped my leg like he did yours, or looked my way with those come-play-with-me eyes, either."

"Shut up, he'll hear you. There was no groping. No bedroom eyes. And he's too young."

"Not for what I had in mind." Lasha looked at Andie's face and laughed. "Not for what you had in mind, either."

"Shut. Up."

"Why don't I go watch your offspring kick some tween butt until you're strong enough to stand on that horribly injured foot." Lasha moved off as the baseball hottie dropped to his knees. "Make sure you get his number, Andie, in case you need him to reimburse you for crutches or something."

Later, she would kill Lasha for embarrassing her this way. Right this minute she had better things to do. Like soak in every detail of the specimen kneeling in front of her. Nice, round muscles filled out his shirt. Great shoulders and pecs did it for her in a big way. This man had both going on. He lifted the injured leg to his lap again, seating her foot on the fly of his uniform pants. She stared at her toes, willing them still, when all they wanted to do was jump free of their strappy sandals and wiggle against his crotch. Good god, she needed to end this before she did something stupid.

"That's cold." Reflexively, she tried to draw her foot away. He held it and the ice pack in place while looking up at her. With his level of hotness, the ice would be water in minutes. Boiling, even.

"Your friend is right, we should exchange numbers."

"I'm not going to sue you for the price of ibuprofen tablets, don't worry." The motion from his chuckle shifted his shirt. A hint of ink on his finely shaped chest peeked out at her. Tattooed men ranked highly in her personal fantasy time. Bad, meet worse. She was so toast.

"I like these shoes. Sexy."

And things just got toastier. "Not your size, sorry."

"I prefer them on you." He winked and swiped one finger across the high-gloss, hooker-red polish on her big toe. "You have very pretty feet. Nice toes."

"Thank you, I grew them myself." She hadn't flexed her flirt muscle in years, but it sprang into action. Pheromones and adrenaline rushed her system, sending heat to her unmentionables and a chill to her nipples. Strange how the body worked. And utterly fantastic.

After inspecting her toes and the injury a couple minutes more, he met her eyes again. "Keep the ice on for ten minutes. I've gotta go, I'm playing on the other diamond and my game is about to start. But you should call me later. For ibuprofen, cold packs, a foot rub, whatever you need. I deliver, 24/7."

"A foot rub—are you a registered massage therapist or something?"

"Strictly amateur. But I do more than feet, and I guarantee satisfaction."

Well that about sealed it. The toys were coming out tonight. The big ones. "Thanks, but I think I'll survive."

"I'm going to worry about this beautiful foot unless I see for myself that it's improving."

Andie couldn't take her eyes off his mouth as it stretched into a glorious, open grin. He had nice, straight teeth. Really white too. Probably a non-smoker, one of the criteria on her wish list. She had no business sizing this guy up. He couldn't be more than thirty-two. Thirty-three at most. Way too young for her.

He pressed a scrap of paper into her hand, letting his fingers linger a little longer than necessary. "My number." Another sizzling smile later, he was walking away, backward.

She set the ice pack aside and stood, taking a tentative step toward the chain link fence beside the diamond. Pain shot up her leg and she winced. He stopped and she waved him to keep going. "I'm okay." She was so not okay.

He shook his head. "Call me, I'll come over and ice it for you."

"What if it's the middle of the night?" Wow, she did not say that in front of all these respectable family types.

"I'll be lying awake thinking about those pretty painted toes anyway."

Andie glanced around. No one had heard the exchange, everyone was intent on the game. Her son's game. Where her attention should be, instead of flirting with a strange man, regardless of how hot he was. Much as she wanted one more gawk, one more sexually laced comment, she kept her eyes on the juvenile baseball players wearing Jell-O green. But she wouldn't soon forget the major player in gray and black.

Want to read more?

GAME PLAN is now available.